D0292242

FINAL ACT

Recent Titles by J.M. Gregson from Severn House

Lambert and Hook Mysteries

IN VINO VERITAS
JUST DESSERTS
MORE THAN MEETS THE EYE
MORTAL TASTE
SOMETHING IS ROTTEN
TOO MUCH OF WATER
AN UNSUITABLE DEATH
MORE THAN MEETS THE EYE
CRY OF THE CHILDREN
REST ASSURED
SKELETON PLOT
FINAL ACT

Detective Inspector Peach Mysteries

PASTURES NEW
WILD JUSTICE
ONLY A GAME
MERELY PLAYERS
LEAST OF EVILS
BROTHERS' TEARS
A NECESSARY END
BACKHAND SMASH

FINAL ACT

A Lambert & Hook Police Procedural

J.M. Gregson

This first world edition published 2016
in Great Britain and the USA by
SEVERN HOUSE PUBLISHERS LTD of
19 Cedar Road, Sutton, Surrey, England, SM2 5DA.
Trade paperback edition first published
in Great Britain and the USA 2016 by
SEVERN HOUSE PUBLISHERS LTD

British Library Cataloguing in Publication Data
A CIP catalogue record for this title is available from the British Library.

ISBN-13: 978-0-7278-8604-0 (cased)
ISBN-13: 978-1-84751-726-5 (trade paper)
ISBN-13: 978-1-78010-787-5 (e-book)

All Severn House titles are printed on acid-free paper.

Severn House Publishers support the Forest Stewardship Council™ [FSC™],
the leading international forest certification organisation.
All our titles that are printed on FSC certified paper carry the FSC logo.

Typeset by Palimpsest Book Production Ltd.,
Falkirk, Stirlingshire, Scotland.
Printed and bound in Great Britain by
TJ International, Padstow, Cornwall.

This, my fiftieth detective novel, is dedicated to my eldest son John, who has been a great help in times of trouble and a steadfast supporter throughout.

ONE

'Shoot the buggers!' said Sam Jackson. He spoke without emotion but with utter certainty. He was used to being obeyed.

His deputy sighed inwardly and blanched outwardly. Ernie Clark knew that his role was to exercise caution, to bring a little balance into their activities. 'I think we need to use a little discretion over that.'

'Discretion is bollocks. I didn't become a successful producer through discretion.' Sam removed the huge cigar from between his teeth and tapped an inch of whitish ash into the ashtray beside him. He didn't read many books, but he'd read about Hollywood and Samuel Goldwyn at MGM and decided Goldwyn was the man he wished to emulate. Television and not the cinema was Jackson's world, but his image was that of the movie mogul, and his method was to hire and fire like old Sam and to ensure in every way he could that his word was law around here.

Ernie Clark said, 'The British like subtlety. They prefer the puzzle of a whodunit to wholesale violence. They don't relish too many shootings or too much blood on their television.'

'Screw the British!' Sam had done quite a lot of that in his time, though he was slowing up a little now. A continual string of nubile girls presented themselves hopefully to him for auditions and the casting couch was one of the Hollywood features he had enthusiastically imported into Britain. But fifty-four years, seventeen stones, an insistently increasing girth and last year's heart attack had moderated his lubricity. Or, as he put it succinctly, 'made him use his dick more selectively.' He waved his cigar in the wide, vague arc which was all too familiar to Ernie Clark. 'We sell in forty-nine countries, so the British can go screw themselves.'

His deputy sighed again. This was a ritual they went through about once a month. His role was to put the economic arguments, but his boss wasn't really interested in any debate. Jackson was by no means as stupid as some people thought him, but he felt it necessary for his image to wave his cigar and assert his vulgarity. Clark said patiently, 'The money which finances the Inspector Loxton series is largely British. The series is set in Britain and our initial target audience is British. It is the audience figures here which help to sell the series around the world.'

'So give 'em what they really want. Reward them for their loyalty. Let the women drop their knickers and let the men who shag them get blasted to kingdom come. Sex and violence: it's a universal formula, that; it works anywhere in the world!' Jackson waved his cigar again and smiled his satisfaction; Sam Goldwyn must surely have said things like that in his heyday.

'That approach might work in a different series, boss, but not in this one. We have established a rather more sedate kind of mystery and we have a loyal following. If it ain't broke, don't fix it.' Ernie could bandy clichés with the best of them, when he felt it necessary.

Even Sam Jackson could not ignore the voice of commerce. 'You reckon? You think we can keep the viewing figures without blood and gore and bare buttocks?'

'For the Inspector Loxton series, yes. It's built around puzzles, not blood and tits and bums, Sam. We have our murders, of course, and they can be gory if you want that, but the main interest is the whodunit one. Our audience is interested in how Loxton unravels the mystery, not in him blasting the villains concerned off the face of the earth.'

Jackson nodded the reluctant acceptance he had always planned. He'd still get a few drawers to drop in a more private context, if he hadn't lost his touch with actresses. But the latest Loxton mystery would unlock itself in the traditional manner. A hardheaded businessman lurked beneath his determined vulgarity. 'OK, Clarky, on your own head be it. Where we going for this one?' As producer, Jackson left Clark to determine locations, but took the responsibility to set up everything else necessary for successful filming. He did that with an efficiency which surprised those who saw only his cigars and his coarseness. The success of the series meant that his budget had increased and things were easier now, but he knew that every day saved in the compiling of an episode added many thousands of pounds to the profits.

'I've found us an ideal area in Herefordshire and Gloucestershire. Nice little hamlet which we can cordon off easily for shooting, lots of green English countryside all around to add to the charm. Not too far from where we've filmed before but very rural. We shouldn't be troubled by the crowds of curious spectators who slowed us down in the last series.'

It was one of the penalties of success that interested fans gathered around the shooting locations. An enterprising coach company had even begun tours of 'Loxton country' around the original Oxfordshire setting.

Jackson nodded. 'How's the casting going?'

Clark knew what was expected of him here. Jackson nowadays employed others to do most of the recruiting, but he retained overall control of casting. He liked to interview females for minor roles himself. One of the perks of power, though no one acknowledged it openly as such. 'Most of the major roles are ongoing and we continue to use the people we've had in them from the start. There's a publican's wife and a couple of small waitress roles which we haven't cast yet. I thought you might be able to help us with those.'

'Sandra Rokeby, you thought.' Sam was studiously low-key. Rokeby had begun her career as a curvaceous page three bimbo. She had progressed from that to appearances in low-key British comedies where she usually managed to remove most of her clothes. She was well into her forties now, but she retained the kind of buxom presence which would still bring audience interest in a smallish role.

'Yes. She'd be another well-known name for us. And rumour has it that she hasn't been offered very much lately. She might be glad of the exposure we could give her.'

Jackson leered his delight in the double entendre. 'I'll see her if you like. Do what I can to recruit her to our gallant enterprise.'

'That would be useful, boss. See what your persuasive tongue can do for us.' He stared carefully out of the window on that.

Sam Jackson wrote 'Sandra Rokeby' in large careful letters on the pad in front of him.

Ernie Clark waited until he had his boss's attention again. 'Nearly everything else is in place. I thought we could call this one something like *Horror in Herefordshire*. People like a bit of alliteration. We should begin shooting at the end of April. I'm trying to arrange some advance publicity for us. If we get the locals involved we should be able to get some television coverage as we move into the area.'

Three months later, Chief Superintendent John Lambert was waiting to see his chief constable. Not many things made Lambert nervous. He realized now that a chief constable who was thirteen years his junior was one of them.

Even as a chief superintendent, you didn't meet your chief constable very often. The public demanded nowadays that their senior bureaucrats should be perpetually available to them, ready to comment on whatever might seem to be even vaguely within their province. All aspects of human behaviour seemed nowadays to demand some kind of reaction from chief constables. CCs had to be careful to give due attention to whatever statements they made. One of the consequences was that they weren't in direct touch with their senior staff as they would have been thirty years ago, when John Lambert was a fresh-faced and eager young detective constable. Gordon Armstrong, chief constable of Gloucester and Herefordshire now for thirteen months, conveyed these thoughts to Lambert as they stirred their coffee and smiled warily at each other.

These were the preliminaries; John Lambert was wondering still why he had been summoned here. Was it for congratulation or for reprimand? He couldn't recall any recent occasion for either of these. He nibbled his ginger biscuit and waited.

Not for long. Gordon Armstrong had allotted twenty minutes to this meeting in the midst of a crowded day and he needed to get on with it. He hoped Lambert recognized the honour accorded to him by the china crockery and the coffee and biscuits. He summoned a smile and said, 'You like the theatre, I believe, John.'

'Christine and I visit the one at Malvern three or four times a year. They provide some interesting productions.'

'They do indeed. I try to get along there myself, whenever I can make the time for it.' He shook his head sadly. 'And now some prominent actors are to be not on the stage and distant but among us. Asking for our assistance, indeed. Have you heard about the latest case of Chief Inspector Loxton?'

Lambert was immediately and instinctively cautious. 'I've read a little in the local press, sir.'

'The *Gloucester Citizen* got quite excited about it. And legitimately so, I suppose. The actors and extras and the whole supporting television crew will be bringing employment and a little harmless excitement into our area.'

'I suppose they will, sir, yes.' Play a straight defensive bat; don't risk any shots unless you have to. Let this smooth young bureaucrat make the running. Don't take the initiative until you know what he's about.

'Causing quite a stir among the locals. They'll be filming in your area, I'm told. Within just a few miles of Oldford.'

'Will they want roads closed off, sir? Because if they do I'm sure—'

'Oh, it's nothing like that, John. We can safely leave the traffic police to cope with all of that, can't we? This is something altogether more original and more worthy of your talents.'

This must be the googly coming up; John didn't know which way it was going to turn. He didn't like the continued use of his first name. In his considerable experience that rarely prefaced good news. 'My talents are limited and severely concentrated upon CID work, sir. I flatter myself that I'm a good taker of villains, but my career has been narrowly focussed upon serious crime and its perpetrators, sir.'

'Come, John, you're too modest, I'm sure! It can't have escaped your notice that even the national press has taken to calling you the "super sleuth". You're something of a celebrity.'

'I'm sure that's an exaggeration. And it's not my doing; I've always shunned publicity rather than courted it. I still do.'

'I know you do, John. But success brings its own challenges. And I am about to present you with one.'

The bouncer at last. Time to open your shoulders and smite it out of the ground. 'I don't want anything to do with the media, sir. I'm not good with the media. We have trained officers to do that.'

'We have indeed, but they're not suitable for every occasion. Sometimes the task demands a public figure. And the police service has to consider public relations now more than ever. We get a bad press too often. When we get a chance to remedy that, we have to take it with both hands.'

Just as my attempt to hit this ball out of the ground is being caught with both hands on the boundary, Lambert thought desperately. He became apologetic when he should have been vehement. 'PR really isn't my strength, sir.'

'But they've asked for you by name, John. Sometimes our fame seeks us out, whether we wish it or not.' Armstrong smiled benignly, giving his chief super the impression that he was quite enjoying this.

Lambert sighed. 'What exactly is the nature of this assignment, sir? It's possible I could suggest someone more suitable to carry it out.'

'There can be no one more suitable than our local "super sleuth", John.' Armstrong beamed broadly and his junior was quite certain now that the younger man was enjoying this. 'The company who are to film this murder mystery on our patch want you to help them. It won't require much preparation on your part.'

'I don't even watch the Inspector Loxton series, sir. Crime fiction on the box irritates me. They make so many mistakes on procedure. They say things and take actions which would never be allowed to us.'

'I think he's Chief Inspector Loxton now, John. My wife is a fan of the series. And I suppose it provides harmless amusement for people who might otherwise be making mischief. But I'm glad you feel as you do, because it makes you the ideal man for the job.'

'What job, sir?' Lambert asked dully. It was another bad move, but he sensed now that he was beaten. Perhaps he might at least be able to cut his losses if he was quick upon his ageing feet.

Gordon Armstrong smiled as if savouring some private joke. 'The company making the series wants you to appear with the producer or director, John. To compare and contrast real crime with the way it is portrayed on television – with particular reference to their series, of course.'

'Of course indeed, sir. Their series is all that concerns them. This is no more than a publicity exercise on their part. Advance notice of the series, with real coppers portrayed as PC Plods compared with their brilliant and intelligent shortcutters.'

'You're absolutely right, John, as usual. But we mustn't be negative. This is an opportunity to put the point of view you just expressed so forcefully. You can talk about the problems of real policing and the way they are airily dismissed in television crime dramas. I can think of no one better qualified to do that.'

'Bullshit, sir! With all respect.' He'd never expected to use that word to a chief constable.

'But the public needs our bullshit, John. Provided of course that we shovel it to them with skill. And when you put your mind to it, I'm confident there is no more efficient shoveller in the service.'

Sir Bradley Morton broke wind. Loudly, lengthily, luxuriantly.

The sound reverberated round the lounge of the guesthouse, then rumbled away like departing thunder. Sir Bradley waited for a reaction from the only other occupant of the room and received none. The younger actor clenched his newspaper a little more firmly and remained resolutely behind it.

The theatre veteran tried not to sound disappointed as he dropped automatically into the words he had uttered hundreds of times before in similar moments of release. 'Better out than in!'

David Deeney lowered his newspaper now. He stared critically at his senior. The lion of the theatre badly needed a haircut, he decided. The grey hair stretched untidily over his collar at the back. The old rascal was looking older, he decided, and not entirely healthy. His nose was redder and slightly more bulbous than when he had last appeared with him two years earlier. That wouldn't matter too much for this television enterprise: the make-up girls would handle it. They would need to earn their money where Sir Bradley was concerned, but no doubt they were well used to ageing celebrities and outsize egos.

No doubt his customary over-the-top performance would be well received in *Herefordshire Horrors*, which now seemed to be the agreed title for the latest episode on the Inspector Loxton series. There had been plenty of deaths in previous episodes, but no one took them too seriously. A rising number of well-known theatrical names had now lent their presence to the series. Sometimes they had to deliver the lamest lines with tongues firmly in well-practised cheeks, but the considerable public who watched them seemed to accept that almost eagerly. The ratings were good enough to ensure high salaries for guest appearances and the repeat fees from around the world provided steady pensions for some eminent names who were now being offered fewer roles.

'Always better out than in.' Sir Bradley repeated his observation, as if he were offering a final chance to a lesser actor who had failed to come in on cue.

'That could be a subject for lively and extended debate,' said David, making an elaborate show of opening the window and gazing towards the late-afternoon sun over the Malvern Hills. He had a better part than Morton's cameo role in the latest murder mystery. Nothing could take that away from him, so he would tolerate the old boy. He might even pick up a few theatrical anecdotes for the autobiography he envisaged later in his career, though most of the ones he had heard so far were second-hand and over-rehearsed.

'One of the classic English dramas begins with a fart,' said Sir Bradley with a benign smile. It was good to display your knowledge of the stage to the ignorant young. They weren't steeped in the theatre and its lore, as people had been in his day.

'*The Alchemist*, you mean,' said David loftily. "Thy worst – I fart at thee." I'm sure that first line got the audience's immediate attention in its day, but it's difficult to shock anyone nowadays. We did our own production of *The Alchemist* when I was at RADA.'

Morton tried not to look put out. 'Some people can fart at will. I never mastered that.'

'For which relief, much thanks,' David answered.

'Le Pétomane. That was the chap. Stage name of Joseph Pujol, the noted French flatulist. That doesn't mean he played the flute, you know.'

'No. It means he made a living from farting. Used to play well-known tunes – he could do "O Sole Mio" and the "Marseillaise", so he must have been both a romantic and a patriot. He could also blow a candle out from several yards away. Great favourite of Edward VII, apparently, when he was Prince of Wales.'

Sir Bradley was considerably put out, though he strove to conceal it. It was always a bugger when your amusing stage stories were taken over by some upstart who should have more respect for your standing in matters of histrionic history. He said sullenly, 'Must have put a great strain on the poor sod.'

'He lived from 1857 to 1945, I believe. Eighty-eight years old when he died, so it couldn't have done him much harm. Friend of mine did a dissertation upon him. Used to breathe in through his arse and then expel the air again, so I suppose strictly speaking he wasn't farting. His stage assistant must have been grateful for that.'

'Lived a little too early, didn't he? He'd probably get a BAFTA for it nowadays.'

'Even a knighthood, perhaps, in these enlightened times.'

Sir Bradley stared at him darkly, but failed to catch his eye. 'No one would raise an eyebrow about farting on stage nowadays. Not with all the kitchen sink stuff your generation is so fond of.'

David Deeney was forty-four. He said firmly, 'Kitchen sink had been and gone long before I was on the scene.'

Morton nodded slowly. 'I remember Larry doing Archie Rice in *The Entertainer*, you know. Caused quite a stir in theatrical circles, that did.' He'd never spoken to Olivier in his life, but the great man had been dead for many years now and it seemed safe to claim a certain kinship with him. Most people brighten when they think of their youth, and actors more than most. Brad smiled fondly as he said, 'Rex Harrison used to fart a lot, you know, in *My Fair Lady*. That was involuntary rather than controlled, though. Julie Andrews told me all about it.' The famous songstress had actually recounted it in a distant television interview, but Bradley thought it was long enough ago for him to retell it as a personal confidence.

'I didn't know that, no.'

'Oh, yes. Julie as Eliza took great care not to get downwind of him, as you might say.' He chuckled at the excellence of his wordplay. 'Her mum and dad were great troupers, you know. Ted and Barbara Andrews. Stalwarts of the music hall and radio in their great days, before the box took over. They introduced Julie to the stage as a teenager. Well before your time, lad.' It was before Morton's as well, but sufficiently vague in period for him to embrace hearsay as part of his personal experience.

David said, 'Television is a more intimate medium. I don't suppose there'll be any call for farting in the next few weeks.'

It was an attempt to bring the old man back to present concerns, but Sir Bradley wasn't ready for that yet. 'I could never fart at will,' he said soulfully, wondering if he was admitting to a major theatrical weakness. 'But I've been able to belch at will throughout my adult life.' He demonstrated, moving smoothly from piano to fortissimo. 'It was a great advantage when I gave my Toby Belch at Stratford. I felt the bard would have been proud of me. Even when we transferred to the Barbican, I retained the facility. The London critics were duly impressed. And I brought the house down when we toured in the north.'

'I suppose the provinces weren't used to such sophistication in those days.'

Morton's glare had minimal effect. 'What do you think of Martin Buttivant?'

'Ah.' A lengthy pause in which the two very different men became mysteriously at one. Weighing the merits and demerits of fellow actors was always fun, and usually most fun of all when there were only two of you. There was always the possibility of giving offence when you were in a large group – people had their own axes to grind, their own contrasting experiences to draw upon. But when there were just two of you in guaranteed privacy, you could be outrageously and deliciously bitchy.

It wouldn't prevent you being a shameless bootlicker in the presence of the man himself on the morrow, of course. The theatre was a precarious profession and you had to look after yourself, whatever hypocrisy that dictated in the moment. Everyone understood the strange rules of the profession. You were never less than marvellous to your face, but that didn't protect you from what people said in your absence. That was why actors trusted no one and were perpetually insecure. Bathed in the most extravagant of tributes, they still wondered as they towelled themselves down what their admirers really thought.

'Martin Buttivant believed his own publicity,' said David Deeney. 'He wrote his own reviews of his shows when he was an amateur and convinced himself of his enduring excellence.'

'He lacks versatility.' Sir Bradley nodded sagely. 'He quite certainly couldn't produce a fart to order. Not even a decent belch, I'm sure.'

'I expect Martin thinks it's not strictly necessary in his role as a chief inspector,' said David, as if striving to be fair. 'But it would add something to his CID ambience. We haven't had a decent CID belcher on the box since the late lamented Warren Clarke played Dalziel.'

'Adam Dalgliesh omitted the possibilities of wind altogether,' said Morton wistfully. 'Written by a woman, of course. They tend to ignore the full rich possibilities of human physiology.' He farted again, almost reverently, it seemed.

'I expect we shall all be dutifully sycophantic to Buttivant in rehearsal, nevertheless. We wouldn't be here without him, would we?'

Sir Bradley grinned sourly. 'Probably not. The man's a turd, but even turds have their uses. I had other offers, but the turd won through. The money's quite good, isn't it?'

'Very handsome.' David wondered how much more the flatulent knight was getting than he was, but you didn't discuss such things. The sordid business of finance was best left to agents. And a knighthood meant things, in this business, however much it was mocked behind the scenes. It added to your price per line on telly, as well as upping your fees and opportunities for interviews. Perhaps he would be a knight one day, if he lived long enough and appeared in the right things and played his cards right. It couldn't be impossible, if this scatological buffoon could make it. Visions of chat show hosts laughing dutifully at his anecdotes swam for a moment before Deeney.

'Funny business, death,' said Morton reflectively.

Deeney came reluctantly back to reality. 'Lucrative, though, as far as chaps like us are concerned. We wouldn't have this particular assignment without it. Thank heavens for the incurable public curiosity about death.'

'I've done your Ibsen and your Chekhov,' Morton boomed sententiously.

'And done them well, by all accounts,' said David dutifully.

Morton nodded his agreement. 'These fellows are profound. I suppose that's why we come back to them. But the one thing that you can guarantee is that if you give your audience a murder, on stage or film or telly, old Joe Public will want to know whodunnit.'

'Which is why we're all here sampling the rural delights of Herefordshire,' David pointed out.

Sir Bradley nodded aristocratic approval and emptied the last of the bottle of claret into their glasses. He raised his slightly fuller one to the height of his noble brow. 'To murder!' he said theatrically.

TWO

Rank counts for much in the police service, even in these egalitarian days. John Lambert didn't go much on rank, but he decided that in this extreme case discipline and the natural order of things must prevail.

Detective Chief Superintendent Lambert made an executive decision: Detective Sergeant Hook should be the man who chatted informally on television with the producer of the Inspector Loxton series, Sam Jackson, MBE, and the star of the series, Martin Buttivant. Bert Hook was one of the very few working policemen who had completed an Open University degree. Lambert pointed out to anyone who would listen that his sergeant's literary credentials must surely make him the appropriate person to engage in a wide-ranging discussion of real policing with the producer of a popular fictional crime series.

Hook's reaction to this argument was not recorded.

Central Television were delighted to record and transmit what their presenter described as 'these light-hearted exchanges'. It would provide useful publicity for the series, a few days before shooting began on the latest Inspector Loxton mystery, of which the title was now confirmed as *Herefordshire Horrors*. The star of the show, Martin Buttivant, came into the studio with his deliberately larger-than-life producer. The actor knew his role here; his blue eyes sparkled humorously between narrowed lids, beneath hair which was too long for a policeman but immaculately and expensively styled to please his host of middle-aged female admirers. He and Jackson sat back in their chairs and smiled with practised ease at the cameras.

Bert Hook tried to do practised ease, but failed. The other two seemed totally relaxed, totally unconscious of the cameras, which seemed to be examining him like baleful and all-seeing eyes. It didn't help when the presenter of this afternoon chat show introduced him as an oddity. 'Here we have that almost unique thing among practising policemen, a detective who is also a considerable and much respected intellectual. Detective Sergeant Hook not only collars dangerous criminals and locks them safely away from us; he also has a distinguished degree and has studied English Literature to a high level and with distinction. He combines a practical knowledge of the reality and the grimness of modern crime with an almost unique capacity to estimate popular fiction. No doubt DS Hook will be anxious to point out to us the flaws in what Sam Jackson and Martin Buttivant present to us, whilst they claim it to be the genuine article.'

Sam Jackson regarded both Hook and the presenter with mounting distaste as the latter delivered this prepared spiel. He'd been warned that there was strictly no smoking on set; he had nevertheless brought a large unlit cigar with him as a stage prop. He pointed it now like a pistol at each of his adversaries in turn as he said, 'We're in the entertainment business, dear boy. We put bums on seats and aim to keep them there. Even when these bums are in their own homes and perched upon comfortable armchairs.' He beamed suddenly and unexpectedly at the man beside him. 'Martin Buttivant here is not a copper but an actor. He happens in my opinion to be a bloody good one.'

Sudden and rapturous applause from the audience. Buttivant smiled modestly, allowed the noise to run its course, and held up an arresting hand as it began to die. Then he spoke in rich and measured tones. 'Remember please that all of us here are on the same side in this. No one respects our policemen and policewomen more than I do. All of us sleep more easily in our beds each night because of their actions. When occasional evidence of corruption or rank inefficiency is exposed, I am the first person to say that this represents the exception rather than the rule. I am sure the audience will agree with me when I say that we are lucky to have men like Detective Sergeant Hook working on our behalf.'

The applause this time was more sporadic and uncertain, as if the clappers were anxious to recognize his very worthy sentiments rather than support the integrity of the nation's police force. Literary parallels flooded unbidden and unhelpful into Bert Hook's surprisingly fertile mind. They were not helpful to him. He felt not like Hamlet dominating the Danish court but like Wodehouse's Gussy Fink-Nottle thrust on to the stage to present prizes. He said sternly, 'Mr Jackson and Mr Buttivant are quite right. They present crime fiction, not real crime, and they do so highly successfully. I am not here to criticize them.'

The presenter leapt upon this like a hungry lion upon raw meat. 'Oh, but you are, DS Hook. That is exactly why you are here. Because unless the adventures presented to us under the mantle of Detective Chief Inspector Loxton have some convincing basis in fact, they will not be able to carry the credibility which the public demands. Reality is a necessary background, a stage setting, if you will, to the mysteries which are so entertainingly unravelled for us upon the nation's television screens each Wednesday evening.'

Hook didn't want to get involved in the errors of detail in the series; he sensed that would lead him into arguments he couldn't win. He smiled as blandly as he could and said, 'The public doesn't always demand realism. The James Bond films have been one of the great commercial successes of the modern cinema, but no one really believes that spies and secret agents behave as the central character in the series does.'

It was not the presenter but Sam Jackson who replied to this. He said wistfully, 'You get lots of naked flesh in the Bond films. That makes people less critical. A screen filled with curvy female ass dulls the critical faculties.' That last bit was worthy of the great Goldwyn himself, Sam thought; modesty had never been a troublesome virtue to him. His sentiment brought a delighted roar from the audience, part hilarity and part shock at his directness at this hour of the day. His use of the American 'ass' seemed somehow more shocking than its British equivalent.

The presenter wriggled uncomfortably, a warning from his producer shrilling in his earphone. He needed to shut up Jackson, who was waving his cigar and threatening further indiscretions. 'I think everyone accepts that the Bond films are high-spirited romps. But somehow one expects television crime series to have a more solid basis in fact. The stories are of course fictional, but one expects Inspector Loxton as the central character to be convincing as a British policeman. Martin Buttivant, as the man who has played this role now for several years, would you not agree with me on this?'

'Oh indeed I would, James.' Always memorise the name of your interviewer and use it as frequently as you can without grovelling. Buttivant was by now a veteran of TV interviews as well as a popular actor in a hit series. 'One of the first things I did when I was offered the part of Ben Loxton six years ago was to attend my local police station and immerse myself in police procedure for two whole days. It increased my respect for the police service. May I say again that our police officers, male and female, do a wonderful job in circumstances which are often trying.'

'More trying than those presented in the Inspector Loxton series, perhaps. Would you not agree, Detective Sergeant Hook?'

Bert started a little. He had been happy to see the exchanges diverted away from him. Now the spotlight had been turned abruptly back upon him. He said stiffly, 'The public wants a solution within the time slot allotted to the series. It is inevitable and understandable that television will cut a few corners. Police procedure is boring. It is inevitable, probably desirable, that much of it will be ignored in favour of a simple storyline.'

'So you're telling us that the Inspector Loxton series is unrealistic, that it ignores most of the problems you meet in real policing?' Controversy is the lifeblood of television discussion; the presenter had mouthed this mantra at the beginning of his career and never forgotten it.

DS Hook sighed and fingered his collar, which suddenly seemed unaccountably tight. His weather-beaten, unremarkable face resembled that of the old-fashioned village bobby who remained cherished by the British public long after he had disappeared. He was a much shrewder man than he appeared and that was a professional advantage to him: criminals regularly underestimated Bert Hook and suffered for it. But on television, an amateur amidst three professionals, he was at a decided disadvantage. Detective Chief Superintendent John bloody Lambert had landed him with this and he'd get his own back in due course. He said a little desperately, 'In most murder cases, we proceed by elimination. We have to explore many blind alleys before we eventually find the one which leads to success. Blind alleys do not make for good television.'

Sam Jackson decided that he had been excluded from the discussion for quite long enough. He pointed his cigar at Hook's chest and said accusingly, 'Are you telling me that women don't drop their drawers in real life?'

Bert was thrown by this non sequitur and no doubt looked baffled for a moment. He tried to smile as he said, 'We meet all aspects of human life in the police service, Mr Jackson. Ladies underwear is one of the less disturbing ones.'

Hook got his first small laugh from the audience on this, but Jackson went on as if he hadn't spoken. 'Because I'm telling you they do. Most of what men do is motivated by what women have inside their drawers, and criminals are no exception!'

This brought another roar of appreciation and the presenter decided to heed his producer's urgent instruction to cut his losses. 'Well, this has been a most stimulating discussion and I thank you all for taking part. We shall look forward even more to the latest Inspector Loxton investigation, now that we are assured that it has a solid grasp of the realities of criminal life and the campaign our policemen conduct against it. Thank you DS Hook for your valuable insights into real crime. Thank you Sam Jackson for your usual trenchant viewpoint on the essentials of television fiction, and thank you Martin Buttivant for your view from the centre of this and for the pleasure you have given us over the years as an actor.'

Bert Hook spent a little time with them in the hospitality suite before returning to the duller world of police procedure. Unlike Jackson and Buttivant, he had refused to indulge in booze before the programme. He now accepted the generous gin and tonic thrust upon him as his reward and listened to Sam Jackson enlarging enthusiastically upon the luscious physical attributes of Sandra Rokeby, who was to make a guest appearance in the *Herefordshire Horrors* episode. 'Does she have a big part?' Bert asked innocently. He smiled weakly through the Rabelaisian explosion this brought from Jackson, who then asked him if he would like to appear as an extra in this locally based episode.

Bert declined the offer as politely as he could, trying not to envisage John Lambert's horror and derision at such a diversion. He slipped away from this histrionic world as swiftly as he could, feeling its pretensions and its deceptions totally alien to his normal way of life. His wife Eleanor would want to know all about it when he arrived home, but for himself he was glad to be rid of the false glamour and back in the real world.

Crime and punishment were the basis of his existence. They were solid realities of life in twenty-first-century England, however a nineteenth-century Russian novelist might have treated them. He was glad to be rid of these posturing thespians.

DS Hook had no idea on that bright spring afternoon how swiftly and brutally he would be thrust back into professional contact with them.

Sandra Rokeby had never claimed to be a top-quality actress. There had been occasions, indeed, when she almost denigrated her talents, indicating that it was her other, less aesthetic and more physical attributes which had endeared her to the public.

She had passed over thirty years from outrageous page three girl, with her twin claims to fame displayed liberally and at every opportunity, to popular but limited actress. Practice does not always make perfect, but it usually leads to improvement. She had been in more or less continuous employment now for twenty-five years and had appeared with some of the most respected of the nation's thespians. Despite her dumb blonde and curvaceous status, Sandra was certainly not stupid. She would never become one of the nation's acting dames, but she had acquired a certain competence. She had also shown a readiness to send up herself and her image, and that endeared her to a country which believes that no one, not even an actress, should take herself too seriously.

Sandra was now regarded with sentimental affection by the English public. Her brazen use of her body in adolescence had become with time a loveable vulgarity, rather than something to deplore and shut away from the children. There was every possibility that if she maintained her public exposure – which she proposed in every sense to do – for another generation or so, she could become in old age that mysterious but much-admired British phenomenon, a national treasure.

She had spent most of her life in cities, but she now breezed into this predominantly rural area with a characteristic exchange with the local press. The young reporter who handled show business for the *Gloucester Citizen* was putty in her hands, the first of several double entendres with which this experienced, jovial woman set about enriching his copy. She interviewed him – that was emphatically the order of things – in her hotel room in Cheltenham. She was here unaccompanied, to play an important role in a successful drama; Sandra assured him unsmilingly that she took her acting very seriously.

Having but the haziest sense of theatrical history, the reporter consulted his notes nervously and then was unwise enough to ask Miss Rokeby if she regretted the decline of the repertory theatres which had formerly provided such a useful grounding in acting essentials for the more mature members of the profession. She withered him with a glance from her wide and vivid blue eyes and asked him quite how old he thought she was. As he stumbled into an apology, she assured him that the reps had gone before she was even a babe in arms.

'I was thrown in at the deep end, ducky! You pointed what you had at the camera and trusted that they would make the most of it.'

'And you never had any complaints!' Her interlocutor attempted a humorous recovery.

'No, rather the reverse, in fact. I was invariably asked for more. Cleavage covers a multitude of acting deficiencies, when it is properly deployed. I turned my twin weapons upon any opposition. If that didn't work, I turned my back upon them in a very short skirt.' She demonstrated the tactic to him now and was gratified to seem him gulp in the manner which had become familiar to her over the years. Men were suckers for female flesh: it upset their judgements in ways which were very useful indeed. You just had to choose your clothes and your moves carefully as your flesh aged a little.

The young man had enjoyed too sheltered an upbringing to be a successful showbiz correspondent. His brain ceased to function as the aforementioned cleavage was lavishly and movingly displayed. Miss Rokeby leaned extravagantly forward, then back again, inspecting her thinly deniered thighs as her skirt rose with the movement. He looked desperately around the luxurious bedroom, jettisoned his prepared and useless list of preliminary questions, and said, 'You're here alone, Miss Rokeby.'

'So far I am, dear. You never know what life will throw up, do you?' She gazed with a smile at the double bed behind him. 'I've always been an optimist, and on the whole life has been good to me.'

'Is it a big part you have in *Herefordshire Horrors*?'

Sandra beamed at him affectionately, emphasising how attractive she found his innocent naivety. 'You'll have to wait and see, won't you? It wouldn't be fair to reveal things in advance. But perhaps I'm not cut out for small parts.' She leaned forward again, threatening for a moment to reveal not just cleavage but the full glory of the assets which had made her name.

'I believe some great actor said that there are no small parts, only small actors.'

'Did he, indeed? Well, that's reassuring for me, since I've never had small parts and I don't intend to be a small actress.' She laughed a little, encouraged him to join her, and concluded the interview on that thoughtful note.

Four days later, Sandra Rokeby was preparing to be briskly professional. All the publicity hypes were over and shooting had begun. This was the first day on location and she was here to do a job and to emphasize to everyone else involved in the enterprise that they should be equally single-minded. She had a youngish man in tow; she had a reputation to keep up, after all. But he would disappear very shortly now; she would be thoroughly professional when the time came for that.

Shooting on location was a complicated business. You had to admire the industry and thoroughness of the people who set things up, the people who got scarcely a mention in the credits which flashed quickly across the screen whilst viewers turned their attention to other things at the end of the television transmission. A canteen had been set up to feed everyone, from technical staff like cameramen and make-up girls through the extras and the bit-players with a couple of lines to the stars of the show, the actors who were household names to the many fans of the Inspector Loxton series. Everyone had to be fed and watered, everyone had to be kept as happy as possible in the often trying circumstances of location shooting.

You never knew what the weather would be like, for a start. The director might insist on waiting many hours until conditions were suitable for an outdoor scene, or he might reschedule the order of scenes at short notice to take account of prevailing conditions, whether wet or dry, whether warm or exceedingly cold. Actors had to be hardy and adaptable souls when shooting on location rather than in the studio.

There were, as everyone knew and most people simply accepted, considerable, sometimes volcanic, temperaments involved. These were indulged more than usual in popular television series, because it was almost impossible to replace an actor in one of the principal roles without strong objections from the public and serious blows to the make-believe which lies at the heart of all drama. We are telling a story, writer and director and actors admit, but the more real we can make the story seem, the more it will convince and the more our audience will enjoy it. The naïve among the public, a surprisingly large section of the audience, identify the actors with their roles as if they were not actors at all. Any unscheduled departure of actors from senior roles damages that willing self-deception which audiences undertake.

Studio shooting is relatively easy. It is when you are on location that the major problems of the artistic temperament usually occur. So producers do everything they can to keep these considerable and highly important egos happy. Most of the major players in the Loxton series were well-behaved, by the standards of television drama. They were, in the jargon of the profession, 'good troupers'. In truth, most of them had been glad of the work when the series started and were even more glad of it now, when Inspector Loxton was a greater success than anyone had envisaged.

Martin Buttivant, who played Loxton, had been a reliable but small-time player when the original series had been commissioned six years ago. As he would still confess when pressed in interviews, he 'knew which side his bread was buttered on'. He was grateful to writer, director and producer for making him into a star. Even Sir Bradley Morton, the greatest name in this present episode, was glad of the work at his age, though he would never admit that, even to himself. Even Sandra Rokeby, imported at considerable expense and with maximum publicity for this Herefordshire-based episode, was glad of the exposure, as she assured any cameras trained upon her with a wink and an amiable leer.

Nevertheless, everything was done to keep the major players happy when shooting on location. They needed privacy to prepare for the ordeals of shooting – they needed the equivalents of their own dressing rooms which they would have been allotted in any of the nation's great theatres. They were provided with small but luxuriously equipped caravans for their rest, recreation, and preparations for the ordeals of performance. They must be happy if they were to be effective before the location cameras.

The allocation of caravans was keenly studied by the members of the cast. Some of the lesser players had to share, but to be given a caravan at all was a clear and desirable mark of status. It established an order of precedence and set you above the lesser players who had to do their crosswords in the communal restroom and eat with the others in the canteen where excellent food was prepared and constantly available on a self-service basis. The catering was put out to tender and the food was almost invariably good, because producers had realized a long time ago that theatrical armies like military ones march upon their stomachs.

It is not easy to keep up morale on a grey day with scudding rain. The director eyes the skies and hopes desperately for the conditions he needs for a three-minute outdoor scene. Despondency can spread quickly through the motley group of personalities assembled solely for this peculiar purpose of perpetrating fiction convincingly in an English countryside which refuses to cooperate. Sir Ralph Richardson, that realist among actors, thought that, 'The art of acting consists of keeping people from coughing.' The harassed deputy producer of *Herefordshire Horrors*, watching the clouds drop lower and the rain fall more steadily, thought that on this day it would be an achievement to keep his actors from coughing.

The principal players had their own caravans and might be expected to be reasonably content: they were after all experienced in the trials of days like this. Ernie Clark toured the site dutifully to make sure that all was well. Sam Jackson's name might be stamped all over this, might be on everyone's radar when it came to awards, but it was his deputies who put themselves about and strove to solve a multitude of problems on such difficult days like this. Those were the rules of the game and everyone understood them. Jackson raised money and gave the show business fraternity in press and television the quotes they desired. He was a 'character', the British public had long ago decided. People wouldn't forget about the Loxton series whilst he was around. But it was his deputies who picked up the pieces and kept things going on harsh days like this.

Ernie Clark appreciated that and did his best in trying circumstances. Actors frustrated by the elements are not the most understanding of mortals. The extras were collected in the canteen and as contented as could be expected. 'Resigned' would have been a more accurate epithet. They were huddled together in groups, drinking record numbers of coffees and becoming intensely repetitive about the British weather. They were mostly experienced, which made them philosophical about days like this. The cream buns from the local bakery had gone down well; Ernie made a mental note to double the order for the following day.

Martin Buttivant had his latest mistress in the caravan with him. Ernie Clark knocked carefully and waited dutifully until bidden to enter. The pair were only talking: Martin would have regarded it as unprofessional to engage in congress when he might at any moment be called upon to act. Buttivant was pleasingly realistic about his acting abilities, recognising himself as competent but by no means brilliant. He knew he was lucky to have secured the Loxton role and even more lucky that the series had become an international success, though of course he would never voice those thoughts publicly. Modesty was all very well on occasions, but it should never be carried to extremes.

He introduced Juliet Cooke as 'an old acting friend who had dropped in to renew acquaintance'; Ernie Clark was happy enough to go along with the fiction. 'Doesn't look as though we're going to film much today,' Martin said, stooping a little to glance through the caravan window at the incessant rain.

'John suggested we might alter the sequence and do that scene near the end in the thunderstorm. There's only you and David in it and it involves you getting very wet.' John Watts, the long-standing director of the series, was conscious that he had been allotted only fifteen days for location shooting and that every day was expensive. He needed to make something of even days like this one.

'I'll get my regulation police plainclothes mackintosh out and turn up the collar,' Buttivant promised philosophically.

'We'll tuck you up in bed with a hot toddy afterwards,' said Juliet Cook solicitously.

She was plainly finding it difficult to keep her hands off her lover and Ernie Clark was happy to leave them to it. At least his leading actor was prepared to make the best of a trying day. And Buttivant seemed content; the big thing on location was to keep the larger egos content.

Ernie took a deep breath before knocking at the caravan door of Sir Bradley Morton. A sonorous voice bade him to enter, seeming to come from somewhere beyond the elements themselves, which were not only grey and wet but threatening at this moment to becoming blustery. A little water trickled down Clark's neck as the deep baritone of the oracle boomed from within.

Sir Bradley surveyed him under the eyebrows which had impressed on stage and screen for half a century. 'Come in, dear boy! Sit yourself down and tell me the latest gossip from this rural haven.' He poured a measure of whisky for his visitor, then refilled his own considerably larger glass, adding a generous measure of water to Ernie's drink and a token drop to his own. 'Difficult day for you, this. People getting impatient and making trouble, I expect. We old hands know better than to do that. We're professionals, you see. We've endured many days like this, in our time upon the boards.'

There would be no work from the theatrical knight today, Clark noted. Morton must have almost a bottle of whisky inside him by now. He wouldn't be troublesome, but it was no use asking him to work. Even in some minor scene he would be reeling about, slurring his speech, and delighting the extras, who loved nothing better than a little scandal to take back to the normal living which existed outside this madness of make-believe. Not like Sir Bradley, that: he was usually quite responsible on set. Ernie wondered if he was under some sort of strain. He downed his drink dutifully and took his leave with a sickly smile.

Sandra Rokeby was drinking more modestly in her caravan. She had a young man he had not seen before with her, but there was no sign of what she had called 'hanky-panky' earlier in the week. 'This is Jason,' she said. 'He fancies a theatrical career. I'm giving him a little experience. He's here to pick up whatever he can.' She fluttered her eyes in a way which was by now almost automatic. Ernie gave her a weak smile of acknowledgement, wondering if she ever spoke without a double entendre. He was in truth a little in awe of Sandra. The fact that she sent herself up so consistently didn't mean that she wouldn't erupt with the full fury of a theatrical institution, without warning or provocation. That was the trouble with this profession: people both disguised their true feelings and indulged them, without any forewarning of which was to happen on a particular day or at a particular hour. Still, Sam and he knew things about La Rokeby which would probably keep her in line.

'Jason and I will be perfectly all right in here,' Sandra purred contentedly. 'You can safely leave us to our own devices.' Jason grinned weakly at Ernie. He was out of his depth here and he might sink without trace. But he had solved a problem for the harassed Clark: Sandra Rokeby appeared to be quite content with her lot on this difficult day.

Things, he reflected, were probably as good as they could be on this depressing and largely wasted Monday. They might at least be able to do a couple of shots with the extras filing dutifully into the village church in the late afternoon; he would leave it to the director to explain to them that it was supposed to be a bright day outside the walls of the church and persuade the women to appear in summer dresses and the men in open-necked shirts, however much they might shiver off-camera.

It was three o'clock when Sam Jackson arrived.

The aroma of his cigar went before him, exciting the extras and the bit-part players, filling Ernie Clark with foreboding. Sam's neo-Hollywood voice boomed out as soon as he sighted his assistant producer. 'Time's money! I'm feeding and watering this fucking army! And what's it doing for me?'

All heads turned towards Ernie Clark, who was suddenly centre-stage in this real-life drama. 'The weather is against us, Mr Jackson, as you can see. We hope to be able to shoot a couple of minor scenes before we up sticks for the day. Given reasonable weather during the rest of the week, we hope to be back on schedule by—'

'Hope! I don't finance this expensive bloody circus so that buggers like you can hope! I pay for results, Mr Clark. You know my methods, or you should fucking know them, by now. I pay for results and if I don't get them heads will fucking roll! Is that clear?'

'Eminently clear, Mr Jackson. It's just that you must understand that—'

'Must? Must? Watch your step right there, Mr Clark! No bastard tells me I must do anything. Do you understand that?'

'Yes I do, Mr Jackson. I was merely trying to explain the realities of the situation. There are problems with—'

'Problems! Don't come moaning to me about fucking problems! Problems are there to be solved, man! First rule of filming! First rule of any bastard who is fortunate enough to work for me!'

'Yes, sir. That's understood, but I have to point out that there are difficulties.'

Jackson didn't believe in doing things in private. You focussed on someone and gave him the full and public blast of your disapproval, *pour encourager les autres* as well as to get things moving. He now waved his smoking cigar at the considerable audience of actors, extras and technical staff who had gathered around his forceful entry and shouted, 'That goes for everyone in this ramshackle fucking enterprise! I want results. I'm not interested in fucking excuses! All of you buggers should remember that!'

They filed dutifully away. Sam Jackson watched them go, then muttered more quietly to Ernie Clark, who had felt himself to be a routine straight man in a familiar performance, 'That shook the bastards up, Ernie. That should get things moving!'

Clark didn't see how it would make the slightest difference to what happened today, except that some of the minor figures would feel so apprehensive that they would be unable to perform effectively; that would land him with cuts and re-shoots. At that moment, he would cheerfully have dispatched Samuel Jackson to the furthest and most painful regions of Dante's inferno.

On that wet and depressing Monday, he had as yet no idea what would happen upon the morrow.

THREE

Tuesday dawned bright and clear. There was a God after all for television producers and directors.

The bright spring morning seemed to imbue cast, extras and technical staff alike with a new energy and optimism. No one liked days like the previous one. People had been paid for doing nothing, which in the popular imagination is supposed to be paradise. A day like that wet Monday must be, in the old army parlance, 'a good skive'. Money for old rope, or in this case for histrionic inactivity.

In fact, people in general and actors in particular would rather achieve than skive, at whatever level they happen to be operating. In an overcrowded profession, there is already far too much 'resting'. There had been frustration and the irritability which it inevitably provokes at all levels on that damp Monday, from the unemployed make-up and continuity girls to the principals who were unable to ply their strange and exacting trade. Now there was anticipation, optimism and a desire to put something worthwhile in the can.

By nine o'clock, they were ready to film the single location scene of Harry Green, a reliable bit-part actor who was playing a greengrocer destined to be the first murder victim in the *Herefordshire Horrors* episode. His murder, which took place in near-darkness late at night, had already been shot in the studio. After today, Harry Green would be on his way to other things, or 'resting' if his agent had failed to secure him other employment. This led to problems which seasoned practitioners like Sir Bradley Morton claimed to have foreseen.

Harry's duty in this three-minute scene was to conduct a routine, even dull, conversation with a customer whose face the audience never saw. The grocer was to serve him with Jersey Royal new potatoes and half a kilogram of tomatoes. He was to be non-committal and businesslike through this routine transaction; his dialogue involved no more than the routine British exchanges upon the weather. His only taxing duty was to show a final flash of apprehension as he looked upon the departing back of the customer the television audience never saw, so as to heighten their interest in who this might be and increase their concern for the cheerful and innocent grocer.

The scene had to be shot twice because Harry, impeccable through his conversational duties, overdid the apprehension of the final seconds. Perhaps he wanted to stretch his part with a view to future employment, or had in mind the repeat fees from the overseas showings which everyone had been talking about through the wet Monday. Whatever the reason, Harry Green showed naked fear rather than the merest suggestion of foreboding which the script directed, which gave far too much of a clue to the villainy of his customer.

Sir Bradley Morton, copiously breakfasted and waiting impatiently for a scene of his own, commented wryly and too audibly that Green was supposed to show a flicker of alarm rather than to shit himself three times over. There was a discussion between producer and director as to whether Green's over-acting could be edited out, then a reluctant decision to waste more of this perfect location morning by re-shooting the scene.

Sam Jackson was putting himself about and keeping everyone on their toes; you didn't become a big-time producer without a massive cigar and a mastery of the cliché. He addressed a varied collection of extras, who had gathered to observe him, partly curious and partly awestruck. 'Time's money when you're on location, and I don't want none of you to forget that. You're getting your five minutes of fame and I'm the mug who's paying for it.' He waved his cigar in a vaguely threatening arc which embraced all of them. 'So I want value for money from you lot and no buggering about.'

His pep talks to the more senior members of his cast were no less direct. He told Martin Buttivant, who was only four years his junior, to 'get bloody detecting while the sun shines, lad.' He instructed David Deeney, who was playing an old-school Anglican clergyman of impeccable morals and even more impeccable diction, to 'roll yer "rs" as well as your arse and make the buggers below your pulpit look as though they're interested in this claptrap you're throwing at them.' He even instructed Sir Bradley Morton, knight of the realm and theatrical institution, to 'move about the place as if you care and don't rely on that foghorn of a voice to do everything for you.' He gave Sandra Rokeby an ugly leer as he told her to 'get your finger out and give it the full orgasm today, girl!'

He didn't have much effect upon any of these seasoned pros. They realized that Sam Jackson was operating in the age of the 'celebrity' and that he would do everything he could to foster his image of movie mogul turning his attention to television. It might not be a very attractive image to them, but it seemed to be a permanently beguiling one to the public, who read about it and saw it acted out in public places rather than suffered it at first hand.

Owing to the efficiency of director, cast and back-up staff rather than to Jackson's exhortations, they made good progress through the morning. Sir Bradley, static but sonorous in spite of Jackson's instructions, was excellently cast as the long-term owner of the local manor, who had fallen upon hard times but refused to recognize it. The ageing but well-loved actress who played his wife was a little stiff and occasionally slow in her reactions, because she was in truth now very deaf. But she lip-read well and Sir Bradley enunciated well, so that she was for the most part able to disguise her deficiency. This would probably be her last role of any size or import and there was sympathy for her, even in a profession which depended upon the survival of the fittest. John Watts was an able director, and he saw that he could build in her occasional faltering by simply making the character of the lady of the manor a little more doddery.

They made good progress through the morning, assisted by the fact that Sam Jackson did not emerge from his caravan after his initial motivational outbursts. Sandra Rokeby completed the scene where she met the young man and invited him back to her place. John Watts found her excellent on set, relaxed and able to take direction, secure in her lines, completely professional. She was half sinister femme fatale, half a humorous send-up of herself in that very role. It was almost a microcosm of the whole Inspector Loxton series, which attempted to provide intriguing puzzles without taking itself too seriously or taxing its audience too much.

Watts congratulated Sandra on her performance after they had it in the can and the cameras had cut. 'Just ask me to play myself and I'll do it,' she said with a grin. 'All day and all night, if necessary.'

It wasn't as simple as that, and both of them knew it. You couldn't just put yourself, or even what the public had come to accept was yourself, unthinkingly on screen and be successful. That would emerge as stale and second-hand. You had to give some thought to it, to decide exactly how you would tease and attract the young, good-looking actor who'd been given the role of the naïve young man whom she was beguiling and leading he knew not where. Every seduction, or implied seduction, must have its own dialogue, its own gestures, and its own charms.

John wondered exactly what Sandra Rokeby was like beneath the make-up and that carefully developed carapace of the middle-aged voluptuary. She was certainly intelligent, despite the image of herself she chose to project. She had been imported to liven up this single episode in the series, but she knew what went on around the Inspector Loxton set-up better than most. He'd find a part for her in future episodes, if the decision were left to him.

The ancient village church they had hired for the week photographed well on this cloudless day. There was something timeless about the mellow stone and the arched windows which could only add to the gravity of what was essentially a lightweight series. John Watts doubled the time allotted to the opening shot of the scene and allowed the cameras to dwell appreciatively upon the elevations which had not changed in centuries. You could afford to set the scene without the distractions of human presence when the setting was as agreeable as this. Even viewers anxious for plot development would welcome the build-up of atmosphere.

David Deeney did him proud when he eventually shot the scene inside the church. He presented a vicar who was thoroughly modern in his views, but with a touch of old-style formality in his manner. The extras who were his congregation – or that small part of it which the cameras were positioned to show – had been warned that their role was to pay rapt attention. They had little difficulty in following this injunction, because David as the vicar addressed them directly and compelled their attention. A series of rhetorical questions was asked of them, fully scripted but expertly delivered by the actor behind the dog collar.

Watts was impressed by Peg Reynolds, the young actress who's role was to stay on in the church in the next scene to ask for the vicar's advice and guidance. Her lines were standard and uninspiring, but she had that mixture of vulnerability and independence that the part demanded. Her manner said that although she genuinely wanted to have this experienced man's advice, she would weigh it objectively before she decided whether or not to follow it. The plot demanded that she should be more than a young ingénue, because she would emerge as a suspect in the later stages of the story. She sat in the pew with her head a little on one side, weighing the merits of her mentor and what he said as well as being grateful for his advice.

Peg Reynolds was pretty, with dark eyes and dark hair which dropped neatly to her neck. She had large brown eyes and a wide mouth, with the regular white teeth which were nowadays almost standard issue for young actors of either sex. A smile lit up her face whenever she chose to use it. John Watts was well aware that male judgements could well be swayed by female beauty: he had fallen into the trap himself as a young director; he had even seen some of the more obvious male homosexuals in the profession make bad calls when swayed by an appealing young female face. But Peg was a woman to note and appreciate, he decided, a name to store away for future and weightier roles than this one.

She spoke to David Deeney as the vicar, nodding in the face of his earnest injunctions towards caution, faltering just enough with embarrassment as she revealed her more private thoughts. Then she watched his back thoughtfully as he left, so that the audience knew that she was thinking hard but were left uncertain as to the nature of those thoughts. Her director was presented with the enigma all good actresses leave behind. How much was she simply being herself and how far was she dropping expertly into a role which was in fact quite different from her own personality?

It was an agreeable question and a cheering note on which to end a busy and successful morning. John Watts was still an enthusiast for his profession, despite the multiple instances of human weakness which were volunteered to him each week. He then had an enjoyable lunch and the opportunity for rest and recuperation in the privacy of his own small caravan.

Watts realized suddenly that there was another reason why he was feeling more cheerful and relaxed. He had not seen or heard Sam Jackson for several hours now. That was unusual, probably unique. Was he still on the site? If he was, he would surely be making his presence felt in one way or another. Yet the decibel level at which the producer operated meant that if he was active anywhere on the acreage hired for this location work, John should surely be able to hear him and follow the disturbance he was creating.

Why wasn't he hammering at his director's door at this very moment, complaining that he was wasting precious minutes of this perfect location day when he and the 'idle bastards' he directed should be hard at work? He would have a point, in this case. They might be ahead of schedule for the day, but you needed to use every available moment when you didn't know what the weather would be like for the rest of the week. Sam Jackson might be an obnoxious bully, but it was he who put up the money for all this. He might be showing a good profit on his investment in the Loxton series, but none of them would be here and working without his money.

Watts decided that he would report to his producer before he began the afternoon's shooting. He told his assistant director to assemble the cast members required for a scene with distant views of the River Wye in the background and a herd of Herefordshire cattle with their appealing, vulnerable eyes in the foreground. A minor episode, but a 'scene setter' for which this perfect day offered the ideal opportunity. Meanwhile, he would report on an excellent morning's progress to their formidable producer.

He rapped hard on the door of Jackson's caravan. Perhaps Sam had a woman in there with him. That would explain why he had not been making his presence felt forcibly around the site. John wondered just how welcome he would be, even as the bearer of good news.

He certainly wasn't going to interrupt anything; it took Jackson longer both to conduct and to desist from any sexual activity as his girth grew larger each year. Watts wondered what he would find within the narrow wooden confines of the caravan. Jackson's money meant that he could still have women, but they had lately been coarse and strictly temporary, what Martin Buttivant had described as 'tramp steamers which pass in the night'.

John regretted his impulse to come here now, but he could hardly just go away, having hammered twice upon the door. He turned the handle and opened the door a quarter of an inch. 'Sam, are you in there?' he called tentatively. Silence.

The noisy bugger must have gone off without telling anyone. Uncharacteristic behaviour, but very welcome. They'd get much more done without him, and the bit players would be much less inhibited without his presence. He widened the gap to half an inch and called again and more loudly, 'Sam, are you there?'

He was feeling a little ridiculous now, particularly since some of the extras had noticed his presence at the great man's door. John Watts mustn't look tentative or uncertain to members of his cast. Any hesitation might detract from the absolute and unquestioned authority which a director must carry with him on to the set. He stood upright, called the simple word 'Sam?' imperiously into the space beyond the door, and climbed the steps into the darkened interior of the caravan.

It wasn't until he drew the curtains back that he saw Jackson. He lay slumped on the floor, looking in the moment of discovery like a stricken rhino. John Watts spoke his name again, but he knew now that there was going to be no response. The blackness in the face and the eyeballs which were almost out of the head told him that.

The tie which had killed Jackson was almost invisible in the folds of flesh at his throat. John Watts reached for it automatically and managed to loosen it, trying to ignore the sightless eyes which stared past him at the ceiling. Then he felt automatically for the wrist. There was no pulse, but the flesh was still warm.

FOUR

'I knew him – well, I met him at least. It was only last week that I spoke with him on television.' DS Bert Hook, who was well used to death, could not keep the shock out of his voice.

Detective Superintendent Lambert glanced sharply sideways at him from the passenger seat. 'Nice chap, was he?'

'I only met him for a short time and it was in front of the television cameras. That's a very artificial situation.'

Lambert sighed and repeated patiently, 'Nice chap, was he?'

'No. He was a bloody monster. But I don't understand these showbiz types. I should never have been placed in that situation.' Hook directed the most baleful look he could at his passenger without compromising safe driving.

Lambert grinned. 'You were the obvious man for the job, Bert. Your degree and your literary credentials meant that there was only one man we could send.'

'You pulled rank, you mean. They wanted you but you pulled rank and sent forth a lamb to the slaughter.'

'I've never thought of you as a lamb, Bert. Many other animals spring to mind, but never a lamb.'

'All chief superintendents are bastards. I thought you were the exception.' Hook spoke without rancour, playing out a humorous resentment he had expressed many times already.

'So you didn't take to this man Jackson.'

'On my very limited acquaintance with him, I thought him a bully and a braggart.'

'And now he's dead, in highly suspicious circumstances. Does that make you a suspect, DS Hook?'

'Not if he died this morning, it doesn't. I was in court giving evidence in front of a crown court judge, being told to confine myself to the facts and keep my opinions to myself. Watching a young thug get a suspended sentence when he should have been sent down for a year.'

End of banter. The defects of the justice system and the determination of unscrupulous lawyers to frustrate the efforts of the police to protect the public were too serious a subject for the two men who had worked together for over a decade to continue sniping at each other. Even Bert Hook, considered a dangerous liberal by many of his police colleagues, had no time for young ruffians who exploited the helpless aged. The pair thought about the matter in hand and did not exchange another word on the short journey to the film set location outside Oldford.

As neither man had any experience of the numbers of people involved in the compilation of a popular television series, they were surprised by what they found there. It was almost as though a new village had sprung up overnight, subsuming the old one which had existed there for many centuries. The tower of the old stone church was visible above this upstart community as they drove in, but the low-roofed cottages of the village, which was scarcely more than a hamlet, had been obscured by the swift and temporary erections which housed this small army of actors, extras and technical staff.

Both CID men felt that illogical resentment of the new and the temporary when it intrudes upon the old and the familiar. 'We're getting old, Bert,' said Lambert gloomily, apropos of nothing in particular.

They parked at the edge of the site and walked through to the area almost exactly in its centre which had been ribboned off already as a scene of crime. Lambert had dispatched DI Chris Rushton to take charge here whilst he waited for Hook to return from court, knowing that no one would conduct these initial formalities more efficiently than Rushton. The DI met them now, trim, efficient, emphatically on top of the job and anxious to demonstrate that nothing here had been neglected. 'The pathologist has already been and gone and agreed what was obvious. Death was by strangulation, sir. The meat wagon is available as soon as you choose to give permission for the removal of the body. I thought you'd want to see the corpse in situ before we had it removed.'

Lambert nodded, glanced at the sign above the door which read 'SAMUEL T. JACKSON. PRODUCER', and climbed eagerly into the caravan, feeling that little surge of excitement which always brings adrenalin to the CID man when he is confronted by the most serious crime of all.

There was no doubt that this was murder. The blackening face and bulging eyes with fractured blood vessels told them that. His own tie had strangled him, by the looks of it. The ends of it fell loose at the back of the dead man's neck, where it seemed as though they had been tightened viciously by hand or hands as yet unknown. The rest of the tie was mostly invisible beneath the folds of flesh which fell over the constricted throat of the slumped figure.

Lambert studied the scene with some distaste for a moment. He was well used to death and had seen much worse ones than this. This indeed was one of the less disturbing corpses. There was no blood here. There was the smell of death, but not the awful odours which rose from a body which had lain undiscovered for days or weeks, and no sign yet of the maggots which take over any deceased flesh which is not quickly removed to the morgue. John Lambert was scowling at a problem which was practical and immediate.

'A woman could have done this,' he said soberly to Hook. 'No great strength was required, especially if he was taken by surprise. She simply had to twist the ends of that tie quickly and hard. Perfectly possible for a woman, especially a woman driven by passion.' His hope that half the human race could be immediately eliminated from suspicion died as he took his first look at the victim.

Hook looked at the thick thighs, at the legs flung out stiffly in front of the armchair in which the man had possibly been sitting before his body slumped down to the floor in the throes of death. The shoes were expensive: probably around two hundred pounds, by the looks of the soft tan leather. Luxury always made death more pathetic and somehow more touching, because death reduced the billionaire in a second to the same status as the pauper, with all the trappings of affluence made as irrelevant as day or night, heat or cold. He bent and looked at the nails at the ends of the plump, sausage-like fingers, but did not touch them. They were undamaged and the nails were clean. 'It doesn't look as if the poor bugger was able to put up much of a fight. He was probably taken by surprise, as you suggest.' He turned round to Rushton, who was standing a little awkwardly in the doorway, wondering whether he should simply have left John Lambert and his bagman to form their own first impressions.

'Did the pathologist give any indication of a time of death?'

'No, except that it was recent. But we know that, from people on the site. And the man who discovered the body said that it was still warm. But it's hot in here, of course, so that doesn't mean much.'

Lambert smiled grimly. 'Let's hope that the flesh wasn't so warm that it was alive when that man came in here.' The last person known to have been with the victim was always a suspect, until he or she could be eliminated. It wasn't unknown for killers to report a death they knew would be swiftly discovered, claiming that their victim had been dead rather than alive and healthy when they had paid them a final visit.

Chris Rushton grinned. 'I spoke with the man who found him when we arrived. He seemed shocked enough then. But these people are actors, of course.' He spoke as if they were some strange tribe whose customs were completely unknown to honest Englishmen like him.

At that moment, there was a tentative knock on the side of the caravan, adjacent to but not on the door which Rushton held open. The DI stood back reluctantly and allowed the short, squat man who had knocked to stick his head through the doorway aperture and address Chief Superintendent Lambert. 'Bad business, this.'

'Indeed it is, sir.' Lambert was patient in the face of this unhelpful contribution. Most people hadn't met violent death at first hand before, unless they'd been military or medics. They had to tune themselves in to murder and to the idea that someone close to them, even some friend they cherished, might be involved.

They could only see the head and shoulders of the man who stood outside and Lambert was reluctant to invite him into an area where clues might still be discovered. The face on that head now filled with horror, as it stared between Lambert and Hook at the thing which had brought them here. Then the mouth said, 'This is a location site for filming.'

'Yes. It is also now a scene of crime site. I should not need to explain to you which takes precedence.'

'I understand that. But location filming is much the most expensive part of any television enterprise. And today is a perfect day for it.'

'I'm sorry about that. But this whole site is a crime scene at the moment, in that the person who killed Mr Jackson may still be here among us. Indeed, the statistical probability is that he or she almost certainly is. Have you any idea who that person might be?'

'No. None at all. It could be almost anyone working here today, I suppose.'

'That is the way we have to view things, until we can narrow down the field. That is why the extensive team we have here are busy questioning everyone known to have had access to this caravan between ten a.m. this morning, the last time when Mr Jackson is known to have been alive, and one forty-seven p.m. this afternoon, when his body was discovered. There will be no further filming done here today. May I ask what is your function in this enterprise and what was your relationship to Mr Jackson?'

The man climbed slowly into the caravan, standing as near as he could to the entrance and resolutely refusing to look at the corpse. 'I'm Ernie Clark, deputy producer. Sam was the front guy, but I set all this up. I'll be taking over from him. So it's up to me to get the show back on the road.'

'Not today it isn't. Possibly tomorrow, if we make reasonable progress in the next few hours.' Lambert glanced down at the corpse. 'This is the scene of a serious crime, as you can see for yourself, Mr Clark. It will remain so for the foreseeable future. If my team can complete the taking of statements from people on site today, we may be able to allow you to continue work here tomorrow, but I cannot promise that at this moment. In the interests of progress and efficiency, we should now vacate this caravan and allow my scene of crime team to complete their detailed examination of it.' He rose stiffly and trod the path to the door which had been marked for him by his scene of crime officer, a former policeman who was now a civilian, an experienced man who had conducted many SOC investigations.

Clark retreated before him and stood awkwardly on the flagged approach to the caravan. 'Is there anything I can do to speed up this process? Time is money to us, as I've explained, and we're already behind schedule after yesterday's rain.'

'You could begin by telling us everything you can about a murder victim who is no longer able to speak for himself.'

'No. It seems incredible that we'll never hear Sam again. He was never backward when it came to voicing his opinions.'

Bert Hook smiled wryly. 'We've met before, Mr Clark. In the studios of Central Television a couple of weeks ago. I got the impression on that occasion that Mr Jackson wouldn't take kindly to any form of opposition.'

Clark grinned for the first time. 'That's a polite way of putting it. Sam didn't do discussion, he issued orders. That was part of his image and his image was important to him.'

'He must have been a man who excited opposition.'

Ernie Clark smiled. He liked this weather-beaten copper, who seemed so much more cooperative than the taller, more intense man beside him. 'That might be the understatement of the year. Someone told me this morning that they had a child who made friends easily. Sam Jackson made enemies easily. But he rather liked that. As long as he kept the power in his own hands, he didn't care if he made hackles rise all around him in those whose destinies he controlled. He'd point his big cigar at people and say that if they didn't like it they could lump it – that was one of his favourite expressions. He had a limited but colourful vocabulary. He'd be telling me to shut up and piss off and get on with my work if he was here now.' He glanced towards the now closed door of the caravan and regret showed upon his squat face for the first time.

Hook nodded ruefully. 'We don't like murder victims who make enemies easily, Mr Clark. It leaves us with too many suspects.'

'Who do you think might have done this to Sam?'

'At this moment I've no idea. Have you?'

The challenge was abrupt and unexpected from this innocent-looking source. 'No. I've no idea. Of course I haven't.'

'It's a reasonable question to ask of you, Mr Clark. You know far more about Mr Jackson and his acquaintances than we do at this point.'

'I suppose that's true. It has to be true, hasn't it? But I've no idea who might have done this. I haven't had time to think about it.'

Lambert came in again on that. 'Then give it some thought, please, Mr Clark. You're in a position to know most or all of these enemies you've told us the deceased accumulated easily, so of course we'd like your thoughts on the matter. In confidence, of course.'

'All right, I'll think about it. But when I said Sam made enemies, I didn't mean he offended people strongly enough to make them want to kill him. It's a big step from resenting what someone does or says to you to wanting to kill him.'

Lambert pursed the lips at the bottom of his deeply lined face. 'The transmission from dislike to hatred and then on to murderous hatred. That's a process we've seen in operation many times, over the years. It's a subject on which some experienced CID man should write a thesis. That would have to be DS Hook, who's much more adept at that sort of thing than I am. Of people on the site at the moment, who do you think might well have gone into Mr Jackson's caravan and strangled him with his own tie, Mr Clark?'

Clark swallowed hard. 'I don't know. I can't think of anyone in our business who would do anything like that. We deal in make-believe – that's the actor's *raison d'etre* – and sometimes in melodrama, but real life is different. I can imagine lots of actors and some of the staff who support them talking about killing someone, but it's unthinkable that any one of them would actually do it.'

'Yet it seems one of them did in this case, doesn't it? Perhaps you'd give the unthinkable some consideration overnight, and let us know what you come up with.'

Lambert and Hook went back into the caravan, where a woman was carefully bagging a tiny fragment of soil found just inside the doorway, which might be completely innocent and irrelevant or might be from the shoe of the person who had climbed into this vehicle as an enemy and left it as a murderer. They watched the SOC photographer taking the final pictures of the corpse from every conceivable angle. Then John Lambert gave permission for the 'meat wagon' to ease slowly to the side of the vehicle and prepare to remove the mortal remains of Samuel Terence Jackson, cigar smoker, petty tyrant, and late producer of *Herefordshire Horrors*.

John Watts saw the chief superintendent, who was obviously to be the SIO for this case, arriving on the site with his bagman. A little while later, he watched Ernie Clark's tentative approach to the scene of the crime and the men who were here to investigate it.

He was relieved to see Ernie taking the initiative with the police, who were now thronging the site and questioning even people who had only come here for the day to act as extras. It seemed odd to have so many men in uniforms nodding and taking notes from everyone they could corner. As director of the Inspector Loxton series, he was used to having the odd uniform on set, usually to play the lumpen dullwits who made Detective Chief Inspector Loxton look so alert and penetrating. Watts had to keep reminding himself that the men and women in uniform who were dominating this bright April afternoon were real policemen pursuing a real murderer.

The big cheese would want to see him: he knew it. He was almost insulted when they didn't seek him out immediately. But that was a stupid reaction; there was no room for vanity in this situation. You needed to keep your wits about you, particularly as it was bound to emerge that there had been little love lost between you and Samuel T. Jackson. Eventually that cool, efficient DI Rushton, who looked the part so convincingly that John would like to have drafted him into the series, came and told him that Chief Superintendent Lambert apologized for the inevitable disruption in filming and would like to see him first thing on Wednesday morning. That would be on site here, where they were setting up a murder room.

John Watts knew now what he must do and he had already decided exactly where he would do it. It was some years since he had visited the spot, but he was sure he could find it easily enough, with the help of the large-scale road map he had in his car. But what he had to do needed privacy and he must wait for darkness. Now that the hour had gone forward and they were on British Summer Time, the daylight seemed to stretch unnaturally into the evening as he waited nervously for it to disappear.

Watts dined early at the country house hotel, where he and senior members of the cast were staying, because he did not feel like conversation tonight. There would be only one topic, the sensational death of their producer, and he did not want to be involved in that. He would need to act a part, to seem as shocked as everyone else would be, and he didn't want the strain of doing that. The others were actors, good professional actors, and he was not. That was why he had decided at the outset of his career that he must become a director if he wanted to stay in this business. The director saw the whole scene, not just the small, selfish portions of it which most actors saw. Whatever they might say and even believe about ensemble playing, most actors were immersed in their own roles, their own problems, and the effects they were making. He had the advantage of them in an actual situation, if he could keep his grasp on the whole picture and the events that would emerge against this real-life backdrop.

He sat in his room and looked westward towards the Welsh hills and the sunset. There was not a cloud in the sky now and the sun obstinately refused to dip behind the mountains. He tried to read. He'd found a battered Wodehouse on the shelf of discarded books at the side of the lounge area; suitable light, escapist stuff for his purpose, but the print danced before his eyes and the bon mots and the Shakespearean allusions refused to register with him. The sky was reddening to the west, but the light intensity remained distressingly high. He couldn't go out of his room because he didn't wish to speak to other people. His phone rang twice but he ignored it.

It was definitely dusk when he stole out into the car park. Late dusk, he thought. You needed your car headlamps when you drove and that made it immediately seem darker. He could have used the M50, which was quiet enough at this time of night, but some instinct for privacy drove him on to the A438, which twisted and turned more as the darkness he had craved finally closed in around him and obliterated the pleasant Gloucestershire countryside. He was making for Tewkesbury, where the great battle in the War of the Roses had been fought in 1471; he wondered why on earth that totally irrelevant fact thrust itself into his head now. Because big things were at stake, he supposed; bigger things than he had ever had to deal with before in what he had considered quite an eventful life.

He had a clear picture in his head of where he wanted to go and his memory did not desert him. He found the place more easily that he had thought he would. Piece of cake, really. Only one simple action left now. But don't get over-confident, Watts. Take it easy. Take it cautiously. He parked the car in a bay beside the road and walked the last two hundred yards. There was very little traffic about; he hadn't seen a car for the last two miles. But people might notice you and remember your car, if you parked on the bridge.

He was wearing navy trousers and a black sweater. Ideal gear to pass unnoticed at night. Ideal gear to make you a road casualty, if you didn't keep well clear of any traffic. But no vehicles came as he walked swiftly to the middle of the bridge.

The wide waters of the Severn gleamed silent and sinister far beneath him, as he had known they would. That is why he had chosen to come here. He paused for a minute before he threw it, as if he needed to check for one last time that this was the right thing to do. But God knew he had been over this often enough in his mind. He had rehearsed this moment like a nervous beginner Thespian who had been given a single line to deliver.

He flung the thing away into the darkness, watched it turn briefly over and over before it disappeared into the black. The water was so far beneath him that he neither saw nor heard the splash. The mighty Severn, which had covered so many things over the centuries, received the mobile phone of Samuel T. Jackson and moved quietly on.

FIVE

The weather held for Wednesday. Lambert, arriving early at the site with Hook, gave permission for filming to be resumed, though the caravan where Jackson had died and the ground around it was still cordoned off as a scene of crime area.

It took some time for the mechanics of location shooting to be set up. The first scene was to be a parish council meeting followed by three of the leading suspects conversing outside after the formal proceedings were completed. The scene was swiftly set up in the building designated for it. Gordon Priestley, assistant director, was able, even eager, to do this: there were not too many opportunities for an assistant director to show his metal when the main man was around. But this morning the main man, John Watts, was busy.

Watts was being interviewed by the senior CID man, as he had been warned he would be on the previous day. The case had provided sensational headlines for the day's newspapers. 'TV TYCOON BRUTALLY MURDERED. LOCAL SUPER-SLEUTH TO LEAD INVESTIGATION'. The headlines had occupied most of the front page of one tabloid. Hook did not bring them to Lambert's attention. It would not have improved the mood of his chief. He made sure instead that the chairs were set ready for business at the end of the temporary building which had been hastily imported to the site to serve as the police murder room.

John Watts was not an impressive figure physically, though he carried an air of quiet authority which helped to explain his achievements as a theatre and television director. He also compelled respect among the assortment of histrionic mavericks, male and female, who figured inevitably among the people he had to guide towards the polished television product he envisaged. He was below average height and he stooped a little as he came into the murder room. He seemed to be looking around him as though he needed to check exactly how this scene had been set up.

Watts had deep-set grey eyes which revealed less than eyes usually did, because they remained narrowed through most of the next twenty minutes. He seemed to be anxious to create the impression that it was they and not he who were on trial here, perhaps because he was so used in his working life to taking charge of situations. The small beard he carried jutted two inches below his chin and was fractionally too long, so that it moved disconcertingly each time he spoke. The helpful notes provided by DI Rushton told his SIO that Watts was fifty-two; that was useful because his thin face might have passed for anything between forty-five and sixty.

'You discovered the body.' Lambert made it sound like an accusation. He was uncomfortable among these theatrical types, but in this situation he felt he held most of the cards. The problem was to extract accurate information from people whose business was dissembling. He couldn't see any reason why most of them wouldn't tell him the truth, but would he be able to distinguish the ones who wished to deceive him? There was almost certainly one and quite possibly several of these actor types who would seek to do that.

Watts nodded to acknowledge that he had discovered Sam's body. Then he crossed his thin legs deliberately and precisely, as though emphasising to them how little this interview worried him. 'I discovered Sam's body at one forty-seven yesterday afternoon. I know the time because the uniformed officer who took my statement recorded the time exactly for me.'

'And what was your immediate reaction to what you found?'

It wasn't the question Lambert normally asked of someone who had discovered a murder victim. If John Watts found it surprising, he gave no evidence of that. 'I was shocked, I could not believe the evidence of my eyes for a moment. I was nothing like as calm as I am now, when I have had a whole night to get used to the idea.'

'You handled the corpse.'

The words came again like a second accusation. 'Yes. I felt for a pulse. It was automatic. I suppose I knew from the appearance of his face that he was dead, but my first instinct was to feel his wrist for a pulse. There wasn't one and that confirmed what I already knew in my heart, that Sam was dead.'

'Yes. The fingerprint specialist in the scene of crime team found your prints on his neck as well as his wrist.'

'I don't remember touching him there. I suppose my natural reaction was to try to remove the thing which had killed him, which seemed to be his own tie. But the absence of a pulse told me that he was dead and that any attempt to revive him was futile.'

'And would have resulted in further contamination of a crime scene.'

'You would no doubt think in those terms. I did not. My mind was reeling with the knowledge that the man who had set up the series, the man who controlled all our destinies, was dead in that chair in front of me.'

'That was your first thought, was it? This was the man who controlled all your destinies.'

Watts managed a first thin smile, barely visible beneath his droopy moustache and beard. 'Samuel T. Jackson was prone to reminding us of that fact.'

'You say in your statement that the flesh was still warm.'

'Yes. I shouldn't put too much reliance on that. I was naturally very upset at the time. It was the first thing that struck me, but it may not be very important. You've just pointed out that I touched Sam's neck, which I hadn't recalled myself.'

'But your impression at the moment of discovery was that Mr Jackson had only just been killed?'

'Yes. But maybe I was wrong.'

Lambert nodded. 'That's possible. The windows and door had been closed and the caravan was hot. People who know much more about these things than either of us have told me that Mr Jackson could have died a couple of hours earlier and still felt warm to the touch when you reached him. But it seems you were the first person to see him after his death.'

This apparent non sequitur was added calmly and clearly, as if it was a fact which had to be born in mind. It was in fact designed to provoke a reaction in his hearer and it did that. John Watts uncrossed his legs and bent earnestly forwards. 'I didn't kill him, you know. It was a hell of a shock to me to find him like that.'

'I'm sure it was, Mr Watts. And the sooner we can eliminate you from our list of suspects, the happier we shall be. There are far too many possibilities around for us at the moment.' He sighed a little theatrically – in this context, he rather liked that adverb. 'No doubt we shall be able to whittle the list of possibilities down to a much smaller number in the next day or two. Those closest to Mr Jackson will obviously form a nucleus of suspects for us. We usually proceed by elimination – unless of course a prime suspect presents himself to us immediately. Confessions are always useful, but regrettably thin upon the ground. You're not about to confess, are you?'

'No I'm not!' Watts looked hard at the gaunt face and found no sign of humour there. This wasn't at all the way Inspector Loxton proceeded, and that fictitious creation was the nearest he had come to murder and real detectives before this case.

'Had you seen Mr Jackson yesterday before you discovered his mortal remains?'

'No. He'd arrived here on Monday afternoon. He gave all and sundry a routine bollocking because we weren't shooting when an expensive location had been hired for the filming. Sam knew perfectly well that you couldn't shoot what were supposed to be outdoor summer scenes when it was pouring with rain, but he wasn't interested in reason. A bollocking and a reminder of the money he was spending were Sam's ways of keeping everyone, actors, directors and support staff, on their toes.'

'And did it work?'

It was the first time John Watts had been asked to consider what might seem to an outsider an obvious proposition. Samuel Terence Jackson had always seemed to him and others around him a force of nature, entitled to throw his considerable weight about because he provided the funds which drove forward this strange, erratic and occasionally wonderful activity. 'I suppose it did work, most of the time. Whatever his methods, Sam achieved things. There are people all over this site today who would be less successful, might in many cases not be working at all, without his money and his vision and his drive.'

Bert Hook, who had seen something of Jackson and his methods during his brief encounter with him in the studios of Central Television, spoke for the first time since Watts had entered the murder room. 'Energy and drive I can accept he had. But he was boorish for a lot of the time, wasn't he?'

John Watts weighed the adjective, then nodded slowly. 'That wasn't the word I'd have used, but I have to accept it. I'd probably have said "ebullient", but then I'd got used to Sam over the years.'

'And you didn't want to offend him.'

Watts frowned, then produced a smile which looked a little forced beneath his whiskers. 'I suppose that's true. You get used to being careful in this business. You can't afford to offend the people who have the money when you're an actor or a director. Generally speaking, the people who have the money also have the power.'

'I thought directors had quite a lot of power.'

Watts laughed outright at that. 'How little you know of this business, DS Hook! That makes you a lucky man, in my book. The people who have the power are the producers, who find the funds for a project and set up the machinery for it, and to a lesser extent the casting directors. Unless you are a very well-established actor whom everyone wants to hire, you're dependent on casting directors to provide you with work, as far as television goes.'

'So you don't think directors are powerful people?' Bert was all wide-eyed innocence.

'Directors are hired and fired almost as easily as actors. They have no money and as a result of that very little power.'

'But the job gives you power. You can make or break a production by the way you shape it.'

'I'm grateful to you for saying that. I wish you could convince everyone in our business about it. There are one or two directors who are universally respected and always in demand: your Peter Halls and your Trevor Nunns. Most of us scrape for our livings and are dependent on a success here and there to keep us going and make us some sort of reputation.'

'So the Inspector Loxton series can't have done you any harm.'

Watts smiled and nodded, looking for the first time relaxed behind his whiskers. It made Bert Hook wonder if the moustache and beard were some sort of mask against the world, rather than the theatrical indulgence he had previously considered them. 'It's gained me kudos as a television director, yes. Nothing succeeds like success, and the Loxton stories have sold all around the world. But they're not rated as high culture and people curl their lips if I'm compared with directors at the Royal Shakespeare or the National Theatre.'

'So your destiny was still in the hands of Sam Jackson.'

'Largely it was, yes. Sam provided the money and he did his own casting, so anyone who offended him was vulnerable. He talked about giving free rein to me and to his actors, but if we'd offended him we wouldn't have lasted long. Actors in an established TV series have a certain advantage, because the public gets used to particular faces and doesn't like change. But Sam always made it clear that no one was indispensable. Even Martin Buttivant as Ben Loxton could be written out and replaced, if he got too big for his boots – that was Sam Jackson's phrase. He said that to me in the full knowledge that I would pass it on to Martin if necessary. Probably he used it directly to Martin himself, but if so I wasn't present at the time.'

'You're telling me that this murder victim had lots of enemies.'

'I'm saying we were all dependent on him. That's two-edged. There might not be a lot of genuine grief around here this morning, but you can bet your boots that this site is throbbing with speculation about what will happen to the Loxton series now. Sam might have seemed at times like an ogre, but he was also our bread and butter – another cliché which he liked to throw at us as a reminder.'

'Did you kill him, Mr Watts?'

John could barely believe the question had come so bluntly from that placid, village-bobby countenance. He checked that the man wasn't joking, that he actually expected a reply. The detective sergeant was waiting expectantly with his head tilted a little to one side. 'No, I damned well didn't! I'm trying to give you all the help I can.'

'We have to ask, Mr Watts. It's part of being objective. The one who is the first person to be with a dead man is occasionally also the last one to have seen him alive.'

'You mean that I might have killed Sam and then gone out and told people that he'd already been dead when I arrived.'

'It's a possibility which has to be considered. Especially as you told people immediately that he was still warm when you discovered him. We don't often have that reported.'

Hook's face had suddenly become inscrutable, so that John still wasn't quite sure how serious the suggestion was. 'Let me be quite clear, then. He was definitely dead when I arrived in the caravan. I didn't kill him. I thought at the time that he must have died in the few minutes before I got there, because his wrist was still warm when I felt for a pulse. But it was an unusually warm day for late April and the caravan itself was hot and unventilated, as you've pointed out. So he might in fact have died much earlier. I'm not an expert on these things, as you are.'

He tried to curl his lip sarcastically as he delivered this last thought, to regain a little of the initiative, but Hook merely made a note on the pad in front of him. 'Where were you between ten thirty and one forty-seven yesterday, Mr Watts?'

'Working. I spent most of the time on set, either preparing for shoots or actually directing them.'

'"Most of the time", you say. Did you have any breaks from shooting?'

'Yes. I went to my own caravan a couple of times during the morning. I took a coffee in there for one of them. I wanted a few minutes on my own to think about the scene with the vicar in the church and exactly what I wanted from him and his congregation.'

'Can you tell us at what times you visited your caravan?'

'No I can't! I was busy with the whole business of getting as much done as efficiently as I could whilst the weather held. Location shooting revolves around the director and how he uses time and people most effectively. I can't be precise about when I was alone.' He didn't trouble now to conceal his irritation; it was surely unreasonable of them to expect that he would know the times when he had been alone.

He got no reaction from Hook. The DS made another note and said, 'I expect someone else will be able to pinpoint these times for us and confirm that you did indeed spend them in your own caravan.'

It was a reminder that everything he said would be checked, that it would be as well for him if he concealed nothing and gave them the most accurate account of yesterday he could. He wanted now to convince them of his innocence, whereas when he had stepped into the murder room he had not felt threatened. He said defensively, 'Sam Jackson must have had a lot of enemies.'

Lambert gave him a grim smile and resumed the questioning. 'As you have already indicated to us, Mr Watts. Which of them do you think killed him yesterday?'

'I don't know, do I? I'd have told you by now, if I did.'

'Yes, I believe you would. Unless you are in any way involved in this crime yourself – as an accessory after the fact, for instance. Or unless you have something to gain by withholding information from us.'

'You know everything I know now.'

'That is much the best policy for anyone closely involved in a murder investigation. But you are not quite correct. At this moment, you know far more about other people we have to investigate than we do. By the end of the week, after we have questioned them and checked what they tell us, that might not be so. At the moment, we need you to speculate. What you say need go no further than this room, but we need your thoughts on others involved. The overwhelming probability is that it was one of the major actors, directors or support staff who killed Samuel Jackson. People at a greater distance, like the extras you have here, did not know the victim and had no reason to hate him or to feel menaced by him, though we shall check to see if there are any exceptions to this. You know most of these principals. Which of them was desperate enough to go into that caravan yesterday and strangle Jackson with his own tie?'

'I don't know. I've thought about it overnight and I haven't a clue. It's one thing to say you hate a man's guts and quite another to go in there and kill him, don't you think?'

'I do. But the fact is that someone appears to have done just that. You work with the people who resented Jackson and many of the things he had done. Which of them is most likely to have done this?'

The thin face was quiet for a moment, then shook quickly from side to side. 'This business deals in hyperbole. I can think of several people who might have voiced the thought of murdering Sam, but none who would have actually carried it out. Some of us like a bit of melodrama – indeed, the Loxton series has rewarded it well – but we don't carry it into real life. We're better at producing murderous phrases and murderous rhetoric than at murder, I fancy.'

Lambert stared hard at Watts for a moment before nodding. 'I accept that. But the fact is staring us in the face that there was an exception here. Desperation leads to desperate acts. We need to find out who was feeling desperate.'

David Deeney had calculated it carefully. He wasn't involved in the next two scenes they were planning to shoot. Then there'd be lunch; you had to allow the camera and technical staff who were working continuously a short break. He wouldn't be needed until early afternoon; not before one thirty, he reckoned. He could get to Oxford and back in under three hours, he was sure of that. That would leave him up to an hour to conduct his business there. Ample time, if he moved into action quickly.

The Mercedes sports car was six years old, but he'd looked after it and the mileage wasn't high. It purred softly and discreetly away from the site, then roared more throatily as he accelerated towards Gloucester. It took him a little time to negotiate the ring road round the city, but once he was away up Birdlip Hill he moved quickly and found the roads pleasingly quiet. There were a couple of lorries ahead of him, but he was able to sweep past them on the short stretch of dual carriageway which was available as soon as he rejoined the A40.

As always, he enjoyed driving the Merc. He'd bought it when it was two years old. It had dropped a lot from the original price but it had still been an extravagance. It had been his way of celebrating his contract for the first series of the Inspector Loxton stories. He'd played a dangerous and violent young criminal then, much younger than his real age. But he'd got away with it and had survived for four episodes before he was eventually unmasked and shot whilst resisting arrest. The work this provided, the success of the series, and the consequent repeat fees from around the world had amply justified the purchase of the Merc. He accelerated swiftly past a Ford and a Citroen on a rare stretch of straight road, revelling in the thrust of the seat against his back and the precision of the steering which complemented the effortless power that surged so immediately when his right foot compressed the accelerator pedal.

The traffic slowed as he queued towards the roundabout where the A40 met the A34 on the outskirts of Oxford. But he had known it would be so and he forced himself to be patient as the minutes ticked away. He was at the house within twelve minutes of clearing that roundabout. This home was modest but lovingly cared for, in estate agents' jargon. There was not a weed to be seen in the front garden. It felt very good to him to have someone waiting for his arrival. The familiar royal blue front door opened silently as he moved between the wallflowers and savoured their scent. The guardian of the door wasn't visible; Trevor Fisher was a man who favoured privacy, even guarded it fiercely when he felt it was threatened.

They embraced each other enthusiastically as soon as the blue door was shut behind them, then kissed at leisure before moving through to the immaculate sitting room, where the coffee pot steamed softly upon its stand on the low table. 'You timed that well,' said David. 'Must be some sort of ESP between us.'

'Nothing so exciting. I saw you parking so I made the coffee.'

Trevor worked from home. He was a linguist and picked up plenty of work from local firms as a translator of two languages into English. One of his most lucrative recent commissions was producing English versions of Swedish crime novels, which David Deeney had helped to secure for him through a contact from the Loxton series. Fisher made an effective house-person. Deeney loved the fact that he was almost always there when he came back to the house, a calm constant in the hectic and ever-changing life which was the lot of the actor.

Actors had to be ready to go wherever work was available, as he had explained long ago to Trevor. Oxford was a good base. London, Stratford and the great provincial theatres were accessible from the great university city, which also had its own thriving theatre. Indeed, he had appeared there last year as Edmund in *King Lear*, one of the parts he had always wanted to play and thought he never would. All actors wanted to play villains who were blackly humorous; they never failed on stage. He'd got spontaneous applause at the end of the great monologue at the end of his first scene. Of course he had deplored the applause publicly to his director as interrupting the flow of the action, but secretly he had welcomed it as a personal triumph.

Trevor Fisher had been in the audience, delighting in his lover's success, and no doubt leading the applause. It had helped to cement their relationship, that production. He'd had excellent notices, and while the Oxford Playhouse wasn't Stratford or the National, it was the next best thing. He was being offered more and more television work and his agent was negotiating character roles in films, but the theatre remained his first love, he thought. Nothing else gave quite the buzz which a live audience could bring to you.

They were finishing the coffee when Trevor said quietly, 'Did you think any more about marriage?'

It was a thing he'd raised before and David knew he would keep coming back to it until they resolved the matter. He wasn't in any hurry to embrace it himself, though he definitely saw their relationship as long-term. He simply didn't see any need for the formal bonds of marriage, perhaps because he'd seen so many heterosexuals make such a mess of it. But it was obvious that Trevor wanted it. Perhaps he felt threatened by the high number of gay actors who peopled the profession. That was understandable, David thought, when you looked at the situation from Trevor's point of view. Like many actors, he wasn't very good at considering other points of view.

He said, 'There isn't time to talk now. I'm not opposed to the idea, but it needs careful thought. We'll discuss it properly at the weekend.'

'You should have something to eat before you go back. Even if it's only a snack.'

David glanced at his watch. 'I haven't much time. I mustn't risk being late back. With a bit of luck they won't even realize I've been away.'

Then he realized that he still had the important thing to do. This was something he didn't wish Trevor to share. They didn't have secrets from each other. But he didn't want Trevor involved in this. It would somehow taint their relationship, taint the younger man, and he wanted Trevor to remain the innocent he always had been to him. He looked at his watch again and said, 'I reckon I've just about got time for a quick snack.'

Trevor Fisher was delighted. He was getting enough translation work now to make a steady living, but working from home meant that his life was a lonely one, especially with his partner having to be away so much. 'Cheese on toast,' he said immediately, knowing it was one of David's favourites, and bustled away into the kitchen to prepare it.

Deeney waited until the door shut and then moved swiftly. His holdall was still near the front door, with the washing he had brought at the top of the contents. He slid the trainers from beneath the shirt and smalls and glanced at them quickly. Then he slipped through the door with his body as shield between what he carried and the house. Wednesday was rubbish collection day. The black bin was outside the gate, as he had known it would be when he had planned this visit. He breathed a sigh of relief when he raised its lid and saw that the bin had not been emptied yet. It was usually two or after by the time they reached this street.

He lifted the black plastic bag and slipped the trainers beneath it. Trevor wasn't likely to visit the bin again until the refuse lorry had been and it was empty, but his instinct was to conceal the footwear. He didn't want a conversation about the trainers, not with anyone, and least of all with Trevor. He was back in the house within a few seconds, with his brain telling him inconsequentially that it was a pity the trainers had to be sacrificed whilst they were still scarcely worn.

He was surprised how good the cheese on toast tasted. He hadn't eaten much breakfast in the hotel, and with his mission now accomplished he felt quite hungry. They embraced again in the hall before he left, Trevor's large hands seeming to linger for a fraction too long on his shoulders when he was anxious to be away. The refuse lorry, with its noisy machinery grinding what it received into oblivion, was at the corner of the road as he drove out.

He had been anxious on the journey to Oxford, but he positively enjoyed the return. The Merc was at its best as he cleared the roundabouts and reached the open road of the A40. He waited patiently for the several miles of dual carriageway which by-passed Witney, then opened up the engine and swept effortlessly past a long stream of vehicles. Then he was through Burford and on towards Gloucester and the location site just over the Herefordshire border, exulting in the fresh greenness of the English spring and nature thrusting back into life all around him.

It was ten past one when he drove into the car park at the edge of the site. He found that the parking place he had deserted three and a half hours earlier was still vacant. As he reversed the sports Mercedes expertly into it, that seemed to David Deeney a good omen.

SIX

Peg Reynolds was a sight to cheer even two senior professionals who were determined to move forward quickly on a serious crime investigation. She was twenty-six years old and had large brown eyes; they looked quizzically at the two men who were about to question her. Her hair was black and lustrous, seemingly without any artificial help.

The two CID officers were of course completely objective about her. They thrust to the backs of their minds the thought that this picture of comely innocence could not possibly be guilty of a crime like this one. Until they knew better, she was as likely to be guilty as anyone else they saw today, Bert Hook told himself firmly. Yet her smile was telling him how unlikely it was that she could be in any way involved in murder. He resolved to give great attention to his notebook.

Lambert opened with: 'You have your own caravan here. We've already learned that that is something of a status symbol during location shooting.'

'I suppose so. It's more related to the number of lines you have than anything else, I think. There's an assumption that if you have a certain amount to do, you need a certain degree of privacy to prepare and to recover. You have to remember that the first take is rarely the final one. There's a lot of shooting and re-shooting when you're on location. It can become quite stressful. You need somewhere to rest and consider your part in the scene, especially if you happen to be the reason why they're having to re-shoot.'

Lambert resisted the temptation to say that he was sure she would never be the one who stumbled. He had no expertise in the area and no reason at all to offer such a banal compliment, but this beautiful woman looked also so composed that it was difficult to imagine her stumbling over lines or movements. He needed to disturb that composure if he was to make her reveal anything she might wish to conceal beneath that immaculate exterior. He said abruptly, 'I haven't heard your name before. Is this your first major role?'

She smiled at him, not at all offended, indicating that as an outsider he could not be expected to know the details of her career thus far. 'It's my first major television role, yes. I've done various things on stage, but I wouldn't expect you to know about them. Even my agent has to be reminded of them from time to time. I'm not even sure that it's fair to call this a major role. I've a couple of scenes and then I'm on with the rest at the end. But it's important for me, because this is a successful series and shown at peak times. It will give me exposure here and in the States, which are the key markets for someone like me.'

It was a prepared speech, but she delivered it as if it was freshly occurring to her. Lambert did not respond immediately. He looked hard at her for a second or two, a tactic which often unnerved those not used to police questioning. Peg Reynolds was used to being studied and the scrutiny did not seem to embarrass her. Lambert said with a touch of abrasiveness, 'And now the whole project is thrown into confusion. From a purely personal point of view, the death of Samuel Jackson must be a blow to you.'

The brown eyes widened a little before she nodded understanding. You couldn't expect coppers, who operated in a completely different world, to know about these things, her bearing said. 'Someone will take over. The Loxton series is a great commercial success. There is no shortage of backing for successful projects. It is the original and the experimental which suffer in theatre and television. In the short term, a sensational murder might even help the series. I'm sure I've heard Sam Jackson voice the old showbiz maxim that there's no such thing as bad publicity.'

Bert Hook looked up from his notebook. 'I met Mr Jackson myself.'

'Yes. I saw that seven minutes on Central Television. Excellent advance publicity for us; it was a good idea to get a real copper involved.'

Bert would rather she hadn't seen that exchange; he was sure he hadn't come out of it very well. He said rather desperately, 'Jackson seemed to me a difficult man. I wouldn't have liked to work for him. How did you find the experience?'

'The work is fine. We've got an excellent director and all the established actors know what they're doing. That makes it easier for a newcomer.'

'Did you like Mr Jackson?'

The perfect features relaxed for a moment into a rather strange, humourless smile. 'Not much, no. But I didn't have to like him. I had to play a part and take his money.'

'He had a reputation for boorishness and sexism. Did he give you any personal reason to be offended?'

'"Personal reason to be offended."' She repeated his phrase, weighing its awkwardness with a hint of mockery. 'Did he try to put his hand up my skirt? No. Did he indicate that he would like to do that at some time in the near future? Yes. But it wasn't a problem.'

'It must have been highly unpleasant, though.'

She looked at Bert Hook as if she both liked him and pitied him. 'I haven't always been an actress, DS Hook. Only for the last three years, in fact. Before that, I was a fully trained nurse. I even have a degree in nursing. The publicity people like to throw that in, when they're desperate for something to say about me. It doesn't have a lot of relevance to acting, in my opinion. But it does have a certain relevance to your enquiry. I was well used to handling sexual advances from men in hospital. For the old and the aged, I even made certain allowances.'

Bert swallowed hard, trying to thrust aside the thought that he wouldn't mind having his declining years sweetened by this angel in a nurse's uniform. 'You're saying that you are well used to handling unwelcome advances.'

Another of those tolerant, almost affectionate smiles. 'I'm saying that Sam Jackson wasn't a problem. I've handled worse than him, in my time. Not literally, of course.' An unaffected grin now, an assurance that this ethereal presence could even tolerate a little innocent bawdry.

'You will understand that I have to ask you this, Ms Reynolds. Did you leave your caravan and visit that of Mr Jackson yesterday morning?' Hook thought he sounded unduly, ridiculously, apologetic.

'I share my caravan with Karen Norman. I mention that only because it means there are certain times when we are in there together. Karen plays a secretary and has the odd line in quite a few scenes. But we're in different scenes and we aren't often resting at the same time, so I could certainly have sneaked out and put paid to Sam. But I didn't.'

'Have you any thoughts on who might have done that?'

'Lots of thoughts, but nothing useful. It's as big a mystery to me as the one I'm involved in on set. But more distressing, of course. One doesn't like to think that there is a murderer somewhere among us, perhaps even acting with me on set.' Her intensely serious face broke without warning into a ravishing smile. 'It's rather exciting, though, isn't it? Not for you, because I suppose it's just work for you. But for the rest of us it's rather frightening and rather thrilling.'

Lambert frowned what felt like very elderly disapproval of this. Then he said austerely, 'Keep thinking and keep observing, Ms Reynolds. Your intelligent appraisal of those around you could be most valuable to us in the days to come.'

Lambert looked hard at Hook as the faint smell of perfume lingered in the murder room. 'That wasn't very productive.'

'No. But she's new to the company. I wouldn't expect her to have many ideas on who might have killed the boss.'

'You may be right, although in my view that young lady is quite shrewd enough to have formed her own ideas. I should think she's probably discussed them with other people by now, though I don't know who those others might be. What I meant was that those few minutes weren't very productive from our point of view in assessing the lady herself. I don't feel I'm any closer to knowing whether or not she's a candidate for our killer than I was when she stepped in here. Are you?'

Bert resisted the thought that it was quite ridiculous that that ravishing, patently innocent and cooperative young woman could even be considered as a candidate for this crime. Lambert was a positive Gradgrind when it came to facts, and until you could offer him facts he wasn't prepared to rule out anyone. Hook said, 'She struck me as far too clever to involve herself in anything as desperate as murder.'

Lambert smiled, recognising his bagman's attempt to appear objective in the face of striking beauty. 'She's bright and she's clever; the two aren't quite the same. We shall have to bear that in mind.'

'For what it's worth, I didn't think she held anything back from us, John.'

The subject of these conjectures was already back in her caravan. It was only fifty yards from the murder room, but she was more grateful than ever before for the privacy it afforded her. She needed to think and she was thankful that Karen was on set and she had this haven to herself. But first, while she still had full privacy, she needed to put on her costume for the scene which was scheduled for shooting at the end of the morning. Be ready for professional action before you permit yourself the luxury of more private thoughts.

She stripped quickly to bra and pants, then paused for a moment to look at herself in the full-length mirror which is the most essential item of equipment for actresses. The livid bruising on her upper arm and above her breast was more spectacular than ever this morning. Vivid blue and green now surrounded the black at the centre, where the blows had almost broken the flesh. The multi-coloured skin around the bruises was a necessary part of healing: she knew that. In a few days, or perhaps even a few hours, the angriness of the colours would begin to fade and the skin which had been so perfect would turn again towards its natural colour.

In the meantime, no one must see this. She pulled the long-sleeved blouse she was to wear for the shoot over her head hastily, slipped into her skirt, and became again the Peg Reynolds who would turn heads in the street and on the screen. She felt a little pain as she twisted the upper part of her body, but nothing she couldn't cope with. She was used to not wincing by now when the shafts of pain coursed through her. The important thing was that no one must know about what her blouse concealed, least of all those two experienced men whose business it was to discover secrets.

There was a sharp knock at the murder room door. In answer to Lambert's invitation to enter, Martin Buttivant stepped confidently into the room and contemplated the CID men. He wasn't a man accustomed to making tentative entries.

'Detective Inspector Rushton said that you wanted to see me at around this time. I'm free for the next forty minutes, so I thought I should seek you out.'

Lambert nodded. 'Thank you. You are obviously one of the people who can tell us most about the background to this crime.'

'I am the principal character in a fictional drama. That doesn't make me the person who knows most about a real crime.'

He had the assurance which comes with television fame. Far more than a triumph on stage, television success brings money and power. Achievement on the great stages of the country is still deeply respected within the acting profession; it brings homage, perhaps even veneration. But success on television brings with it a much wider public acclaim and acknowledgement. You become that most glamorous of twenty-first-century phenomena, a 'celebrity'. You are recognized wherever you go. You earn a mysterious access to seats on Wimbledon's centre court, you are picked up by the cameras at Lords, Wembley or Ascot. People even seem delighted to see you there and to highlight your presence, as if it marked out that particular event as being of real importance.

It is difficult not to be affected by celebrity, difficult to maintain the attitudes and standards you had as a struggling young actor. You are central now to a great and successful enterprise. Everyone else involved is conscious that they cannot afford to lose you, which means that they must not offend you in even the slightest of ways. People defer to you in all sorts of things every day. Quite unconsciously, Martin Buttivant had come to expect that people would be deferential.

It wasn't going to happen here. Lambert sat him down in the chair recently vacated by Peg Reynolds and said uncompromisingly, 'You are fifty years old and have played Inspector Loxton for the last six years, during which the project has grown from a minor television series to an international success. You must have known your producer, Samuel Jackson, extremely well. We need all the information you can give us, not only on a murder victim but on those who were closest to him in the months before his death.'

Buttivant stared at him steadily and said nothing for a moment. He was not by nature an extravagant man, but he carried with him by now the trappings of success. His hair was impeccably groomed and his grey suit had a Savile Row cut. He had crossed his feet at the ankles, which drew attention to the shining leather of his shoes, gleaming but obviously also very comfortable. He now folded his arms, allowed himself a small smile, and stared at them unwaveringly with keen blue eyes. His face carried fewer lines than were usual in a man of fifty. He wasn't as tall in life as he looked on screen. Obviously he wanted to look younger than his years. That was not mere vanity: he wanted to play Inspector Loxton for as long as the series went on and for as long as he could look convincing in the role. Bert Hook wondered if men used Botox. Everything was possible in the exotic world of acting.

Buttivant looked perfectly relaxed. Was that acting also, or did he really have nothing to fear from this investigation? Lambert said, 'We've already heard from others that Jackson was a difficult man who didn't trouble to avoid making enemies. Were you one of them?'

The question was a more direct challenge than Martin had encountered in several years – except from Sam Jackson himself. But he didn't propose to tell them about that. He wouldn't show them that he was ruffled. He steepled his hands and put his fingertips together, raising them a little to emphasize that he was giving the matter due consideration. 'Sam and I got on perfectly well. We maintained an effective but purely professional relationship. Detective Sergeant Hook glimpsed a little of that when we met in the studios of Central Television recently.'

It was his first acknowledgement that he recognized Hook and remembered where he had seen him before. Celebrities learned to do that, if they were sensible and did not believe their own publicity. It won them easy esteem among the public: people were flattered when a celebrity remembered their humble presence on a previous occasion and recalled it to them.

Bert Hook wasn't flattered. He said, 'I thought Samuel

T. Jackson rather an odious man on that occasion. I had sympathy with you as a man who had to deal with him regularly.'

'Sympathy is always much appreciated. But in this case it is misplaced. Sam Jackson didn't give me much cause for concern. I was grateful that he wanted me six years ago. But by the time of this death, he was not in a position to jettison me. I am one of the few people on this site today who was pretty well Jackson-proof. I wouldn't dream of saying that if Sam was still around, mind you! It was the sort of thing he'd have taken as a challenge.'

'You didn't like him, did you?' Bert was persistent in the face of the man's panache. He was a murder suspect until it proved otherwise.

'Not much, I suppose. But in the main our relationship was what I called it a moment ago, purely professional. You train yourself not to like or dislike people, when they have the money and the power to hire and fire. I work in an industry where employment is traditionally precarious.'

'But you were fireproof. You've just told us so.'

'Almost, but not entirely. I've also just told you that Sam would have regarded any such assertion as a challenge.'

'So he was a dangerous man. To others, if not to you.'

Martin took his time. It was one of the things he had learned to do since he had become a celebrity. People hung upon your every word; it only conferred an impression of greater gravitas if you delivered them slowly. He didn't see how they could know about his own dispute with Jackson, didn't see how anyone else was going to tell them. But it wouldn't do any harm to give them a little information about others; that would divert their attention from him. 'Sam offended most people. He enjoyed doing it. It had become almost a way of life for him. The difficulty for me is seeing how someone would translate resentment into hatred strong enough to make them kill him.'

'But someone did. That's why we're all here. Tell us what you know. That's your only obligation. It's our job to find out who took it to those lengths.'

'You speak as if I can give you the full catalogue of Sam's offences. I've told you that it was his habit to offend people, but I really know only a fraction of his life. As far as possible, I confined our relationship to the professional.'

Lambert had let Hook do the questioning for some time, preferring to observe the behaviour under pressure of a man he saw as a central figure in the case. He now said with a trace of impatience, 'So begin the catalogue for us, Mr Buttivant. Name the people whom Jackson had recently offended?'

Martin took his time again. The innocent and the confident wouldn't be hurried, would they? 'We couldn't film on Monday because of the weather, but Sam Jackson turned up in the afternoon and sounded off at most people. Very publicly. I remember thinking that if I'd been his director, John Watts, I wouldn't have taken kindly to being told I was neglecting my job in front of the entire cast like that – particularly as the allegation was totally unjustified. There was no way any of us could have been working in Monday's conditions.'

'You have some eminent names around you for this episode. I imagine they wouldn't take kindly to Jackson's approach. What about Sir Bradley Morton, for instance?'

Buttivant smiled, the slightly twisted smile which half the nation had grown to love. 'Bradley didn't like Sam. But strictly between the two of us, he's glad to have secured the part in this episode. It gives him exposure in a popular series, it's a part tailor-made for him, and it will cement his standing as a national institution, not to mention a national treasure. So he took what Sam threw at him and tried hard to smile at it.'

'Has he got previous history with Jackson?'

Martin weighed the matter. He wanted to implicate the theatrical knight more deeply, but he didn't have the material to do that. 'I shouldn't be surprised if he did. The two go back a long way. Bradley Morton was a successful film and stage actor when Sam Jackson was still in his twenties, but Sam already had his first great success and the money that went with it. I didn't know him then, but he was probably already aggressive with anyone who worked for him. If I know him, he'd have been at pains to put Brad in his place, as he saw it.'

'David Deeney?'

Martin nodded sagely. 'Dave didn't like Sam and he didn't

take as much trouble as some to disguise it. Sam was aggressively and by today's standards objectionably heterosexual. He treated women badly at times, but he never troubled to disguise his lust for them. Another facet of that was his hostility to homosexuals. There are plenty of them in our profession and Sam couldn't avoid employing them. But he took every opportunity to denigrate them and he expressed his contempt for them at almost every opportunity. David Deeney didn't take kindly to that. I wouldn't have expected him to. He has a long-term relationship with another man and he's quite open about it. Sam said insufferable things. Women would certainly regard him as sexist and the gay community would very reasonably call him homophobic.'

'Do you think Deeney snapped? This might not have been a premeditated crime.'

An elaborate shrug of the shoulders. 'Who knows? I wouldn't have thought so, but someone around here has done something none of us would have expected.'

Lambert frowned. 'You said women were in danger from his sexist advances. We've already talked with Peg Reynolds. What about other women involved here?'

Martin allowed himself again that half-pensive, half-humorous smile. 'The only other actress seriously involved in the *Herefordshire Horrors* episode is Sandra Rokeby. And Sandra can look after herself. She'd resent any suggestion that she couldn't, if she were here.'

'I imagine that she too has history with Jackson.'

'I'm sure you're right and I'm sure she'll tell you all about it. I can't give you chapter and verse myself.'

He was terser, less relaxed than he had been previously, thought Lambert. It made him wonder what there might be between Buttivant and Sandra Rokeby. He looked forward to meeting the lady who had been a sex symbol when he was still a young man – well, youngish, anyway. 'Who else was close to Jackson? Who else might have visited him in the hours before he died?'

'You've already seen John Watts and Peg Reynolds. You already know more about their movements than I do.'

So they'd been comparing notes and no doubt also discussing

what questions people had been asked. That was inevitable, in a community thrown closely together on a site like this. But it didn't make the police task any easier when people came in here prepared for what you might ask them. 'Who else other than your fellow actors might have gone in there?'

Buttivant gave the matter careful thought. He had scarcely bothered to think beyond the cast; like most of his profession, he found it difficult to regard anyone else as other than secondary to the main action. Eventually his face brightened and he said, 'There's Ernie Clark, of course. As assistant producer, he was close to Sam.'

'Inevitably, I suppose. What was actually his position in the set-up?'

'I don't know what the financial arrangements were between him and Sam – how much he had invested, how much he took out. Sam always gave the impression he was a one-man band, with all the ideas, all the profits, all the cigars. But that was Sam's way. He'd never admit anyone else made any decisions or offered useful ideas.'

'So what exactly does Ernie Clark do?'

'He works very hard, actually. As deputy producers normally do, particularly those attached to Sam Jackson. Ernie was the dogsbody who did the real work around sites like this, as well as in the studio. It was his job to make sure everything was present for shooting to go ahead – cast, make-up girls, cameramen, props, scenery, etc. Even the catering was his responsibility. He had to watch the daily budget. Filming for television is an expensive business, particularly when we're on location. An inefficient producer wastes money and soon puts a project on the rocks. Ernie Clark is efficient. I'm sure Sam knew that, but I never heard him acknowledge it.'

Hook looked up from his notes. 'Did you visit Mr Jackson's caravan yesterday morning?'

This time Buttivant's smile was almost patronising. 'No, I didn't. I knew Sam reasonably well: that was inevitable as we'd both been involved in the Inspector Loxton series for so long. But we didn't socialise much. Unless I had a professional reason to seek him out, I didn't do that. I had no such reason yesterday morning.'

'After a sensational death like this one, there will be much discussion around the site and among your fellow actors. It is inevitable that you will hear facts and suggestions which don't come to us. Please keep your eyes and ears open and report anything to us which seems even remotely relevant. It is your duty to do so.'

'I shall do that. I wish you and your team every ounce of luck. To quote my entirely fictional character Ben Loxton, "Murder is an ugly business."'

It was a conventionally sombre thought. Yet he looked as he left them entirely satisfied with his efforts.

SEVEN

The scene was set beside the stream at the edge of the location. It was here that Sir Bradley Morton performed his ageing libertine act with verve and enthusiasm. It was what he had been hired for, after all. The producer, the director, and above all his indulgent public expected it from him.

They got it in spades. Morton had given either this performance or a slight variation of it several times over the years. By now he was not quite sure how much of the ageing roué was an act and how much was himself. He was vaguely aware that he was in danger of going OTT. He threw in a 'By Jove!' which wasn't in the script and caressed the upper arm of the lady he was beguiling a little more than the stage directions indicated, but she responded well, with the required indulgent smile and bodily actions which said that this was acceptable and humorous rather than offensive.

Sir Bradley was at his core a highly competent actor. He'd never had the depth for the great Shakespearean heroes, but he'd been an excellent Toby Belch and even an effective Malvolio in the past. And his Falstaff had been well received, if not quite the complete critical triumph he now fondly recalled as the years moved on.

He knew what he was doing here and he was familiar with the people acting with him and with his director. He knew his few lines well and he knew by now how to use rehearsals effectively. Today the real thing went off excellently, he thought. The actual performance always brought a little extra zest from people who'd trained for the stage, Sir Bradley maintained. That zest from him would lift those around him, some of whom had only known this strange world of television acting.

There was a little spatter of applause for him at the end of the scene, a louder one when it was announced by John Watts that the shoot was a wrap and that no retake of this scene would be necessary. Sir Bradley was benign. He nodded affably at the other three actors who had been involved and said, 'Good to know I'm not completely geriatric. They always used to call me "One-take Morton", you know, when I was in films.' They never had, but there was no one here old enough to dispute the claim, was there?

He was exhilarated by the work, but surprised how tired he felt when he climbed back into his caravan. He'd have recovered quickly at one time, but it took longer and longer nowadays. That was understandable, in view of what he knew and no one else here knew. He'd keep working, though. It was part of the image, that. He'd said several times in television interviews that he proposed to work until he dropped dead on stage or in a studio, and each time the studio audience had applauded enthusiastically. There would come a time, perhaps quite soon now, when he would no longer be offered parts; that would have ended it all anyway. But he was never going to confess that to the public and for a lot of the time he was reluctant to confess it to himself. Permanence was part of his persona, part of the aura which had converted him over the years from competent character actor into national treasure.

He was feeling better and fully relaxed by the time his visitor arrived. That owed something to the brandy bottle. He'd had a preliminary snifter himself before pouring two generous measures for himself and his new producer. It was longer than he expected before the man arrived, but that didn't matter to Brad; he'd nothing to do for the rest of the day, now that his scene was safely in the can. He'd have a couple more brandies and sodas, but he wouldn't get drunk. He'd never been one of those actors who became unreliable because they were lushes. The work eventually dried up for them as the word got round. It was all right if you were Richard Burton or Peter O'Toole, but lesser mortals simply disappeared. Brad wouldn't have dreamed of admitting it publicly, but he knew he'd never been good enough to indulge himself like that.

Ernie Clark knocked tentatively when he eventually arrived.

He responded to Sir Bradley's imperious command to 'Come!' by entering diffidently and casting a look back over his shoulder at the world he was shutting out. The very action that would excite the suspicion of that world – but then Clark wasn't an actor but an assistant producer, Brad thought. Well, a producer perhaps, now, and as far as this enterprise was concerned *the* producer. Morton gave him a welcoming smile and held out the drink to him as if it were a chalice.

'Cut glass tumblers,' said Clark, rolling the brandy round the bowl and adding a generous measure of soda. 'You look after yourself and your guests, Sir Bradley, even on location.'

'Especially on location,' said Bradley, with a wide wave of the knightly arm. 'One needs whatever comforts one can muster, when one is cast out into a hostile world.' He sipped his brandy contemplatively, raised his glass towards the light to study it, and ran the healing fluid expertly round the wide bowl of the glass which contained it.

'You asked me to come here,' said Clark. 'What is it you want to discuss?' He had a shrewd idea what it was, but he preferred to let the older man make the running. You were always in a stronger position dealing with a request than arguing in support of your own suggestion; it put the other party in the position of supplicant.

Sir Bradley looked anything but a beggar. He was forced to voice his plea, but he would take his time over it. He prefaced it with a review of the situation. 'I was with senior members of the cast last night. Buckets of crocodile tears were being shed.'

'They owe a lot to Sam Jackson. He put up the money which made all of this possible,' said Ernie Clark sententiously.

Morton raised a bushy and expressive eyebrow. 'That is why we all deferred to the bugger whilst he was around. But he didn't like actors. He treated the men like shit and the women like his personal concubines. That is why everyone around here is glad to see him gone.'

'Everyone?'

'Everyone!' The voice which had effortlessly reached the rear stalls and circle for so many years boomed with conviction. 'I don't see the police getting a lot of help round here.

I shan't ask if you killed Jackson, Ernie. It is much easier to maintain a disciplined ignorance if one is innocent of all knowledge.'

'Then I shan't ask you either, Brad. I might feel it my duty to tell the police, if I had genuine knowledge.' Ernie felt like a poker player resolutely maintaining the appropriate face.

'I imagine you're going to do very well out of this.'

For a moment Clark thought the old rascal knew more than he did. Then he realized he was probably merely probing. 'I've no notion what's going to happen. Have you?'

'I've a shrewd idea. The Loxton series will go on. There will be sensational headlines for a few days. There may even be a sensational arrest. None of that will do the series any harm at all, either here or in the rest of the curious world which forms its audience. For a crime series, all of this will constitute helpful publicity. The person to benefit most of all from this death and its aftermath will be the man who was Sam Jackson's faithful deputy, the assistant producer who has now fallen on his feet in a big way – I imagine that's the sort of cliché our late controller would have used.'

Sir Bradley Morton smiled on that thought and broke wind exuberantly. It was a function he obviously enjoyed, despite his instant assertion that: 'I really must stop doing that!'

Ernie wondered how much the old ham knew about the arrangements which would now be implemented. Morton might be more dangerous to him than he had anticipated. 'We shall have to wait and see what happens next, won't we?'

'"Letting 'I dare not' wait upon 'I would', like the poor cat in the adage?" I prefer to shape my own fate whenever possible.'

'It was Macbeth who was taunted like that and reacted with action, wasn't it? I seem to recall that things didn't turn out very well for him.' Clark was pleased to have spotted the allusion.

'Very good, Ernie. But I can't see how this can turn out badly for you – unless you're arrested for murder, of course.'

Clark looked at him hard, then summoned up a sickly smile. 'Someone will be arrested, I suppose. I wonder who. Not you, I hope, Brad.'

Morton gave him a quizzical smile. Ernie had tried to come back at him about the murder, but it had been a pretty feeble attempt. 'Amongst all of us, you're the one with most to gain, I should think. You'll take over the series, won't you? Even if you haven't got enough money in your own pocket, you'll have no difficulty getting finance for the next series. But I imagine the profits from this one and the money that's still pouring in from around the world for the previous ones will take care of that.'

'I haven't even thought about the implications of this for me yet.'

That was patently untrue. Everyone had thought about the personal implications of Jackson's death, and Clark more than most, because he was most immediately affected.

Morton said calmly, 'Things will move forward in a positive manner. You will take over the Inspector Loxton series. You will make good profits from it and be hugely more prosperous than you were. You will have an infinitely more agreeable lifestyle than when you were chased about and insulted by that ogre Jackson. The actors will carry on without the stream of insults that most disagreeable of men brought to our sets. Even I shall be able to expand as I should not have done if he were still around.'

Ernie Clark was immediately curious, though he affected nonchalance. 'How is that, Brad?'

'I shall be able to look forward to taking a greater and happier part in the series. I should not have accepted more than this one-off role in *Herefordshire Horrors* if Samuel Jackson had remained in charge of the project. Now I shall feel free to expand, to develop my involvement and commitment to the series.'

He was behaving in character and enjoying it, despite the fact that he knew these things wouldn't be possible. It was a blatant bid for more roles, or a development of the one he was playing in this episode. Morton spoke as if it were he himself and not Sam Jackson who had restricted his involvement to this single episode. Everyone in the business knew Sir Bradley had been glad of the work in a popular series, though no one had had the temerity to voice the thought.

Ernie said, 'I don't know what the plans are after this one is completed. I haven't spoken with the writer recently. I'll need to discuss things with her, with Sam gone.'

'You will indeed,' said Sir Bradley affably. 'And no doubt you'll wish her to build in a bigger role for me.'

Sir Bradley wasn't looking at Clark. He was staring ahead and slightly upwards, as if seeing the vision of his life ahead and the myriad things it now had to offer him. Ernie said uneasily, 'I can't make any promises, Brad. There are all kinds of things to consider about what happens now and the future to the Loxton series. But if it proves that—'

'It will prove that you need me, Ernie,' said Morton evenly. He looked full at Clark now, his pale blue eyes bright, his bushy eyebrows seeming suddenly larger. 'Believe me, it is much in your interests that I have an important part in your future plans.'

This was virtually blackmail, Ernie Clark thought. Morton was claiming he knew more than he could possibly know, surely. He didn't voice that thought; he needed time to think about this. He stared at the aged knight for a moment, then said awkwardly, 'I must get back to the set. I'll be needed out there.'

They parted with both of them wondering how much the other knew. Sir Bradley had thoroughly enjoyed playing his little game, empty as he knew it was.

Sandra Rokeby did not disappoint. She had been one of Bert Hook's fantasies when he was a young man, oozing physicality in her photographs and quotations for the ex-Barnardo's boy in the year when his hormones had begun to dance.

She eased into the murder room and looked around, displaying her voluptuous contours effortlessly and to maximum advantage. 'DI Rushton told me you wanted to see me. It's only natural that you should, in view of what's happened here.' She was perfectly affable, more understanding than some of their other clients had been, but she contrived to make it sound like a sexual invitation. Or perhaps she did not contrive it, thought Bert. Perhaps such things came naturally and unthinkingly to her after all these years.

He'd checked her age before she came here. She was forty-eight now, but she carried her age easily because she took no great pains to disguise it. Her clothes were expertly cut to display her figure, but they had not the tightness which would have made her seem brazen. She had the bright blue eyes and blonde hair which had always been her feature; bottle-blonde, Bert fancied, but so expertly applied that he could not be sure. There were not the telltale dark roots which he saw on most such heads. Rokeby sat down easily opposite them, crossing her legs to display fine denier nylon, but not as much of her thighs as he had expected. 'Pretty kettle of fish this is!' she said, exuberantly rather than sadly.

Bert had the impression that she was confident with policemen, that she had handled the species before and was perfectly at ease with them. He said as sternly as he could, 'We need to ask you some questions about what happened yesterday. We need you to be as honest as possible and to hold nothing back.'

'I wasn't intending to do that. It's not my habit to hold things back.' She said it quite soberly, yet she made it sound like a sexual assertion.

Lambert had never seen the sturdy and reliable Hook look so like an inexperienced young constable. He took over the questioning himself. 'You're a principal player in this drama, Ms Rokeby. No doubt you will be able to make us aware of what was going on before yesterday's killing and what took place after it among your fellow professionals.'

She smiled at him, apparently weighing his merits. 'I'm a principal player in a fictional drama. I have no experience of the type of real-life drama which was played out a hundred yards from here yesterday. You are the experts in that. We are merely players, waiting upon your expertise in such matters.'

'You are not "merely" players or merely anything else. It is entirely possible that one of the actors committed murder yesterday. You among others are a leading figure in a major crime, unless and until it can be proved otherwise.'

She looked at him steadily for a moment, the lines around her eyes more visible as they narrowed. 'I take your point. I shall do all I can to help you. It will not be much.'

'Someone we saw yesterday or today will almost certainly be attempting to deceive us. If you are to convince us that this person is not you, we need you to be as frank and as full as possible in your replies, as DS Hook suggested.'

'I don't go in for deception.' She uncrossed her legs and inspected her spotless blue shoes. 'Ask away, chief superintendent.'

'How long had you known Samuel Jackson?'

'Must be the best part of twenty years, off and on. More off than on, though. I hadn't seen him for several years before he offered me the part in *Hertfordshire Horrors*.'

'He interviewed you personally for the role?'

'He always did, when he was casting females. One of the perks of the job, he called it. He always hoped it would lead on to other and more steamy perks.'

'Did you resent that?'

'I've been around this business and this life too long to bother myself with resentment. Men try it on with you. Even women try it on, occasionally. It's a fact of life. I can handle it. I can't remember when I last allowed it to upset me. It's a long time ago.'

'But your rejection didn't prevent Jackson from giving you the part?'

'I knew he wanted me for it when he sent for me. I might be a limited actress, but I'm not stupid, and you get better with practice over the years. I can do everything required of me here. I know I can and Sam knew it. He was a shrewd businessman as well as a lecher, you know. He and I both knew I was value for money in the role he wanted me to fill.'

Lambert looked at her hard. It unnerved many people, who were not used to being studied in the social contexts in which they usually operated. Sandra Rokeby merely stared back at him, with no visible sign of annoyance; she was well used to being stared at.

He said, 'With petty criminals, we are able to make some assessment of their characters and motivation ourselves. We have to discover the characters of murder victims through other people. Everyone tells us that Samuel Jackson was churlish and coarse and that he exploited his money and power to obtain things he would not have gained without them. He must have been a man who made a lot of enemies.'

Sandra gathered her thoughts. 'Isn't that just a caricature of your victim? You fasten on the obvious fact that he could be boorish and take everything else from that. People can be more than the face they present.'

'You think so?'

'I do.' The monosyllables were emitted with a quiet certainty. A few seconds passed before she said, 'I am not what I present to the world. I am not the Rokeby Venus, though that did influence my choice of stage name all those years ago. I am a lot more than what I choose to present to the world. I suspect Sam Jackson was too.'

'I take your point and I thank you for it. We want to know as much about our victim as we can, because it will probably suggest who killed him. But I would point out that the image he chose to present – that of the bullying producer who held the power and wanted to remind everyone of that – was the one which seems to have dominated his final days. He had no children, but for all we know he might have been generous and loving to his nephews and nieces. He might have been an absolute poppet to puppies and kittens, but that isn't what characterizes his final days. He was more interested in being a bastard to his cast and his technical staff. And it was in the midst of these people he had deliberately antagonized that he was killed. Do you agree with that view?'

She shrugged her shoulders, causing her famous bust to produce an involuntary blink from Bert Hook's experienced eyes. 'I have to accept it. The facts support it. I just wanted to point out that I've known Sam to be kind, in the past. Even considerate, when he thought his image wasn't at stake. But he generally played the bastard pretty effectively.'

Lambert wondered if she was trying to distance herself from this killing by recalling the human side of the victim. Or was she obliquely concerned to point out that she was much more than one-dimensional herself, that an intelligent, perhaps compassionate, woman lurked beneath the curves? He said gruffly, 'Did you visit Jackson's caravan yesterday morning?'

'Yes. Not to kill him though.' If she thought her admission was a bombshell, she gave no visible sign of it.

'When and why did you go there?'

'Not long after he arrived here. After my first scene on set. It would be about eleven o'clock, I think. I went to give him some publicity shots. They were to be used to promote this episode in the series and Sam had requested them from me. Normally I'd have handed them to the woman who handles publicity, but I thought I'd let Sam have a quiet leer over them – not that they're anything very scandalous. I don't reveal acres of flesh any more. I have to work by suggestion. But I thought presenting them to Sam himself would help to keep up good relations with him; you have to look after yourself in this job.'

'What did Jackson do with the pictures?'

'I don't know. He had them on the table in front of him when I left.'

'The scene of crime team found the photographs. They were in his inside pocket. Was he wearing a tie when you visited him?'

'Yes. A pretty lurid one, as usual. He had it knotted round his neck. But it was a very loose knot. That was the way he usually wore it.'

'Did you see anyone else visit him, or have you heard of any such visit from the people you have spoken with?'

'No. Most people had the opportunity at one time or another, but I don't know of anyone else who went to that caravan. His attitude to actors in particular didn't encourage it.' She paused for a moment. 'I expect Ernie Clark might have gone there. As assistant producer, he had most reason to do so. And if I'd been him, I'd have preferred to receive any criticism from Sam Jackson in private than in public. An audience always brought out the worst in Sam.'

'What about motives, beyond the obvious one we mentioned that Jackson seemed anxious to insult everyone in public, whatever their standing in your profession?'

There was again that measured pause. Bert Hook had the sudden, unexpected thought that he wouldn't like to get on the wrong side of this woman who had been his sex symbol when he was a young copper. People didn't smoke nowadays, but he could picture Sandra Rokeby studying the white smoke rising slowly from a cigarette as she now said coolly, 'I suppose Ernie Clark is the one who will gain most by this. I expect he'll take over as the producer of this hugely successful series and make his fortune.'

'Do you know of any other reason why he would kill Samuel Jackson?'

'No. And I must emphasize that this is entirely confidential. I'm not trying to incriminate Ernie. I hardly know him – don't forget that *Herefordshire Horrors* is my first involvement in the Loxton series. Perhaps people like Martin Buttivant, who've been here from the start, can tell you more about the background to what happened yesterday.'

'Who do you think killed Samuel Jackson?'

'I don't know. I shall be interested to see whom you eventually arrest.'

'Please continue to keep your ears open and give the matter your full thoughts. You're an intelligent woman, Ms Rokeby, and we shall appreciate your input on this.'

'A little flattery never goes amiss, chief superintendent, even with a woman like me who claims by now to be immune to it. I shall do as you say.' She rose and made an exit which was as measured and unhurried as her entry had been.

'Not stupid, that woman!' said Bert Hook eventually. He hoped this fairly non-committal comment would show how unaffected he had been by the formidable female presence whose perfume still hung heavily in the murder room.

'She certainly made an impression on you, Bert.' Lambert smiled benignly. 'What we have to decide as suspicious coppers is whether in apparently being so forthcoming she was trying to cover anything up.'

'I thought she was straightforward and helpful,' said Hook steadfastly.

'Did you, indeed? Well, she's not stupid, then, as you said just now.'

In the privacy of her own caravan, Sandra Rokeby weighed what had happened in the last twenty minutes. She had experience of police investigations, and she knew that these men were shrewd and thorough. But she thought she'd made a decent impression. The important thing was that they hadn't discovered what she needed to conceal.

EIGHT

Scene of crime and preliminary forensic reports did not offer much beyond what was already obvious.

Samuel Terence Jackson had died by strangulation with his own tie. He had been a strong man and would normally have been expected to offer strong resistance. Though only five feet nine inches (1.73 metres) tall, he had weighed seventeen stones and four pounds (110 kilograms) and been drastically overweight and unfit, with a heart disease of which he had already been warned. He had almost certainly been taken by surprise. His necktie had been swiftly unknotted to allow the two ends to be tightened viciously at the back of his neck. He had died within seconds and without the violent struggle which might have left behind valuable evidence as to his killer. There were neither skin tissue nor hairs beneath the nails of the hands he had no doubt raised in a futile gesture of defence.

Various soil samples had been retrieved from the carpet in the caravan and these were being analysed. Lambert was professionally pessimistic about these. They were probably from elsewhere on the site, but unless they could be tied to particular shoes and particular people they were scarcely evidence. In any case, John Watts had discovered the body and Sandra Rokeby had visited the vehicle, along with God knew how many other people they had not identified as yet. It was possible there might be significant soil residue from the murderer's shoes, but it would be almost impossible to isolate it. In any case, he or she might by now have disposed of the footwear they had worn at the time of the killing.

Similarly, the team had collected clothing fibres from various fabrics other than those worn by the victim, but there was no guarantee that they had been left there on the morning of the murder. Since this caravan had been hardly used, it had not been cleaned for two days before the hour of Jackson's death, so various people could have been there quite legitimately, even if the fibres could be identified.

Two blond hairs had been found on the chest of the corpse and carefully preserved; if a leading suspect was identified and a DNA sample secured, these could be tied to the person involved. But presence would only be significant if it had been previously denied. Lambert had a strong suspicion these hairs had come from the head of Sandra Rokeby, who had already told them quite willingly that she had visited a healthy Jackson in the hours before his death. She might have lied, as anyone else they spoke to might lie, but they would have to expose the lies before such things became relevant, even as supplementary evidence.

Forensic experts always emphasize that there is 'an exchange' between murderer and victim at a murder scene, that however careful the murderer may be, he leaves something of himself behind. This is almost invariably true, as retrieval techniques become more and more sophisticated and the most minute traces can be identified and investigated. But two of the major problems of detection are to pin the evidence to the particular person involved and the time to the moment when the crime took place. It looked as if that would be exceptionally difficult in this case.

Without Sam Jackson's capacity for causing alarm and dissension among the people he employed, location filming went smoothly and comfortably. Such, at any rate, was the not entirely unbiased verdict of Ernie Clark, his deputy producer, and John Watts, his director. The day passed almost entirely without raised voices on the site.

They got through a full schedule of filming and were even able to catch up on some of the scenes which had perforce been aborted on the first gloomy day of location shooting. The two men congratulated each other on the progress made and on the better atmosphere they fancied now existed both among the cast and among the much larger and more varied body of technical staff which supported them.

Clark and Watts were certainly right about the major members of the cast. They were much more relaxed with each other without the tension Jackson had brought with his every visit. Now that Jackson's threats and insults had been so abruptly removed, people found themselves reacting to each other rather than to that baleful presence. Two of his major players determined to have an evening together, a thing they would not have risked had the late producer of *Herefordshire Horrors* still been around.

Martin Buttivant and Sandra Rokeby had worked with each other for much longer than most of their fellow actors realized. They had known each other more intimately, too, in the past, though the experiments of youth were now well behind them. But there usually remains an indefinable closeness about former lovers, especially when they have parted on good terms, as these two had.

They were in the same hotel as the others, but they met for a drink in the bar and booked a late dinner, to make sure that their privacy would not be disturbed by the bonhomie of their colleagues. Sandra refused more than one drink in this preliminary session, then studied her companion surreptitiously as he sipped a second gin and tonic. 'Did drink ever become a problem, Martin?' she asked him frankly.

Martin smiled that slightly crooked smile which was his public trademark; it now came automatically to him. 'It threatened to, for a while. There were a couple of years after we finished our liaison when it might have done. But I couldn't honestly claim that it was the heartbreak of losing you.'

'You wouldn't be believed if you did. And it's much better not to try. You were never much good at keeping secrets from me.'

He grinned affectionately now. 'You were far too good at seeing through bullshit. That's probably why we didn't last. I've got better at bullshit since then.'

'There were other reasons. I wasn't as promiscuous as the press liked to imply, but I never claimed fidelity was my strong point. I was convent-educated, as they loved to point out. I felt I had a lot of catching up to do.'

'It didn't do your career any harm.'

Now she grinned, not at all insulted by the implications of this. 'You can choose your partners with discretion without being a complete tart. But you need to think hard before you jump into bed with people. Sometimes mere flirting and the promise of things to come was enough to get me what I wanted, in those days. People seem to expect more for their favours nowadays. Fortunately for me, I'm in a much stronger position to pick and choose than in my early days.'

Martin smiled at her honesty. 'That doesn't say much for me, does it? I was one of your early choices.'

'You were one of my prehistoric choices, my love. You belong to those innocent days before calculation entered into bedding decisions.'

'I expect Sam Jackson was still anxious to bed you, even when he took you on for this.' The mention of that name spelled a return to the real business of the evening, understood but not voiced so far by either of them.

'He was. He got the politest brush-off I could give him.'

'I expect he told you that you wouldn't be getting more money or more work from him.'

Sandra knew when he said that that he'd had the same threats as her. They went into dinner now, taking their time over their orders for starters and main course, each thinking furiously about what they would say to a former lover. Both of them thought nostalgically of that time which now seemed to belong to another life, where they had thought only of each other and the physical ecstasy their bodies brought to each other. A vanished innocence which could never be recovered. But with innocence there had been vulnerability and other forms of damage. Both of them had needed to acquire a carapace of experience and calculation quickly, in order to survive in this glamorous but ruthless world of stage and television.

It was only as a part of fencing for position, of playing for time, that Martin said with casual vehemence, 'Sam was a bastard.'

'An absolute bastard.' She moved a fork beside her plate half an inch left and said as quietly as if it had been a comment on the food, 'I'm glad he's gone.' She glanced up into the suddenly anxious face on the other side of the table and said, 'He knew all about us, didn't he?'

'He knew about our early affair, yes.' Even now, Martin

wanted to be absolutely certain before he committed himself absolutely.

'He knew more than that, didn't he? He knew exactly how we met and what we did.' There was a trace of irritation in Sandra's voice; Martin was not being as frank as she felt she had already been with him.

'Yes, he did. He knew all about our first professional engagement. Well, mine, anyway. You were already earning good money by then.'

Sandra smiled wryly. 'Good Page Three money. Good top-shelf, girlie magazine money. I wanted to get into acting and I wasn't RADA-trained like you.'

Was there a hint of resentment there, he wondered, an assertion that she hadn't had the chances he had and was therefore less guilty in what they had done? After all this time, they had much better be frank with each other. 'Sam knew about the soft-porn movie, yes.'

He'd voiced it at last, where she would have been prepared to talk about it twenty minutes ago, if she'd only received an answering frankness. But he had more to lose than she had, she acknowledged to herself now. He was a bigger star than her, with a different image. If it became public, people would say they would have half-expected it of her, but were shocked that Martin Buttivant should be involved in something like that. The public could be quite startlingly naïve at times. She said comfortingly, 'We used completely different names and we were paid a pittance. The sex was simulated for the most part, wasn't it? Compared with the hard-porn stuff that's openly retailed now, it was almost innocent.'

'All true. And all irrelevant, as far as Sam Jackson was concerned. He knew what the release of the facts would do to our images.'

'And he made it quite clear to me that he would release the facts whenever it suited him.' Sandra's face set in unwontedly hard lines at the memory.

'Me too. He'd no intention of doing anything immediately, because the Ben Loxton series was making him a fortune and he wanted me to feature in it for as long as it was successful. But he was already blackmailing me, in effect. He'd made it clear there would be no rise in salary, however successful the series. If I contested that, he would be happy to release what he called "our little scandal" to the right people at the time of maximum damage for me.'

They changed the subject then, having confirmed what both of them had long suspected, Jackson's knowledge of that enterprise and intention to use it against them when it suited him. They made happier conversation through the rest of their dinner, recalling past times, exchanging humorous stage anecdotes, laughing over some of the many outlandish characters with which their profession was peppered. They relaxed more thoroughly than either of them would have thought possible, though questions and conjectures about the future crowded their minds, and the death which had provoked this meeting was never far from their thoughts.

They were indoor creatures, both of them, used to crowded green rooms and frenzied exchanges within them. But tonight they felt a need for fresh air, for the freer reaches of the natural world outside the restaurant. It was a comfortable hotel on a fine site, as was fitting for the leading cast members in a successful series. It afforded privacy and it was in a secluded place, looking over one of the country's most picturesque rivers, the Wye.

The river was sixty feet beneath them now as they wandered for a quarter of a mile along the deserted lane beside it. It was a still and warm late-spring night; the soft air was welcome on their faces after the heat of the restaurant. Martin took Sandra's hand, then after a hundred yards slid his arm round her waist. 'Like old times!' he murmured softly.

Yet each of them knew that it was not. Too much water had flowed under too many bridges since they had been young and foolish together. They were older and wiser now, necessarily so. But in these magic moments beneath the stars, they regretted the passing of that innocence which they had relinquished together so readily all those years ago. It was so still here that they could clearly hear the noise of the river, running softly over the stones beneath them. As their eyes grew ever more accustomed to the night, the clear crescent moon and the stars threw up the white of the foam beneath them as the water surged over the occasional protruding stone. The waters from Monday's prolonged downpour were still pouring down here from the Welsh hills and the river was flowing surprisingly swiftly on this calm, warm night.

'Do you think Sam would really have done that to us?' asked Martin Buttivant suddenly. It was the first time they had spoken of the man in two hours.

'You know he would,' said Sandra Rokeby softly. Men were always less clear-sighted than women, she thought. Or was that just this man and this woman? 'Jackson was a bastard. Once he had no further use for us, he'd have delighted in humiliating us like that, even if there was no monetary gain in it for him. He enjoyed spoiling other people's lives. It emphasized his power; he was prepared to do anything to show the power he had.'

Martin squeezed her waist, wishing he could lighten things again. It didn't seem right to be exploring such evil in these wonderful surroundings. He turned her gently and they set off back towards the hotel, walking even more slowly in an attempt to prolong the magic of the setting. Both of them knew that this evening wouldn't go any further, that they would separate when they reached the entrance to the hotel. This part of their lives had ended a long time ago.

But each of them felt an enormous relief that Samuel Terence Jackson had now been dispatched from those lives.

Lambert and Hook were in the murder room early on Thursday morning, well before any location filming had begun at the Herefordshire site. Detective Inspector Chris Rushton was there even earlier. He had collated all the statements acquired on the previous day and provided the chief and his bagman with all the background information he could on the two major players they had yet to see.

They elected to interview David Deeney before Sir Bradley Morton, since they were told that he was likely to be the busier of the two actors during the day to come. Deeney paused in the doorway to assess his opponents and the set-up in this room, weighing them coolly and without embarrassment, pausing a little before he took the chair they indicated, as if it were he and not they who was arranging the physical set-up of this meeting. This was what actors called stage presence, Bert Hook supposed, that intangible but essential part of a stage performer's equipment.

It was a little disconcerting, almost a reversal of the normal order of things as far as senior CID personnel were concerned. They were used to ordinary members of the public being a little overawed by the processes of detection, a little disconcerted by the fact the Lambert and Hook studied them without reservation, watching their every move and their every reaction. Middle-class members of the public, in particular, were accustomed to different social mores; they did not expect their every twitch to be monitored and recorded. In their everyday lives, that was hardly good manners. And it was surely rude to stare.

There was none of this social sensitivity with actors. They studied you and made no secret of attempting to divine what you were thinking and where you intended to go. And David Deeney, a quiet-looking man with a neat, conventional hairstyle and brown, unblinking eyes, a physically unstriking man, was no exception. He was assessing them as coolly as they were weighing him. Or at least that was how it appeared to Lambert: it might have been no more than the actor's habit.

Rushton's notes told them that Deeney was forty-four and successful in his profession. He had rarely been out of work in the last twenty years. He was by no means a star, but where others spent much time 'resting', Deeney was in steady demand. Lambert said without preamble, 'Did you visit Samuel Jackson's caravan on Tuesday morning in the three hours before his corpse was discovered, Mr Deeney?'

'I did, yes. It was a brief visit. As far as I can pinpoint the time, it was at about eleven forty.'

He delivered the information calmly but with absolutely clear diction, like a line in a play. It seemed that he had calculated before he came here how he could make the maximum impact with it. In fact, David had originally intended to deny any visit to that fatal caravan – hence his disposal of the shoes he had worn – but had decided after exchanging notes with his fellow cast-members and his director that this would be ill-advised.

Lambert now determined to be equally calm about his receipt of this information. 'What was the purpose of that visit?'

'Sam had asked to see me.' It wasn't true, but he didn't see how they could possibly dispute it.

'About what?'

David hesitated for a moment. 'I should normally say that this was a private matter, but I suppose murder suspends all the rules. Sam wished to offer me more work in subsequent episodes of the Inspector Loxton series.'

'What was your reaction to that?'

A slightly patronising smile, as though to convey how little these men with their safe jobs and their fat pensions knew of the realities of a precarious profession. 'I was both interested and flattered. About one in five of the possibilities of work we are offered comes to fruition, for all sorts of reasons. Theatres are unavailable. Actors envisaged to play major roles prove to be committed elsewhere. The "angels" who provide the finance for theatre ventures decide projects are not worth backing. Of those offers which do develop into work, about one in a hundred is a sustained television success and goes round the world making money. The Loxton series is one of those very rare birds. Of course I was interested.'

'Thank you for the insight,' said Lambert dryly. 'Was anything more specific discussed?'

'No. I said I would need to check other work with my agent, but I didn't see any problems. Frankly, I'd have been prepared to defer or abandon other things, for something as lucrative as this will continue to be.' He raised his hands a little and then dropped them back on to his knees, as if to emphasize the frankness he was offering them.

'Did you like Mr Jackson?'

The query was abrupt, when it came. But he was prepared for it; it was inevitable, once the man had been murdered. 'I had reason to be grateful to him. Almost everyone you have questioned or will question had reason to be grateful to Sam Jackson.'

'That's an evasion, Mr Deeney. I asked if you liked the man.'

The slightest of smiles and a tiny nod. 'I suppose I didn't wish to seem an ungrateful sod when he was providing me with lucrative employment. No, I didn't like Sam. I wasn't alone in that. I expect you've been hard-pressed to find anyone who claimed to like him.'

'Could you summarize the reasons why, please? Remember that apart from a brief meeting DS Hook here had with Jackson, we have no previous knowledge of the man. We are still assembling a picture of our victim.'

'And you are no doubt interested in the degree of dislike or even hatred which we interviewees exhibit to you.' Deeney smiled, emphasising how much in control of himself he was, what a balanced and detached view he held of this business. 'It's very odd, you know, to be part of a fictional crime series about murder and then to be suddenly plunged into the real thing.'

'I imagine it must be, yes. Why did you so dislike our murder victim? Would you say it went as far as hatred?'

David Deeney looked calm and dispassionate, no more emotional than if he had been asked to pronounce on the merits or otherwise of a particular cheese. 'I tried to keep my distance, to maintain as far as possible a professional relationship. I find it best to keep passion out of these things, as far as possible; it only complicates matters and prevents one operating efficiently.'

Lambert wondered if this man was really as calm as he was presenting himself to them now. He was an actor and probably delighted to deceive them. For his part, he wasn't going to show the irritation he felt mounting within him. 'This is all a little vague, Mr Deeney. Can you pinpoint for us exactly why you disliked Mr Jackson and his attitudes? Everyone is telling us that he was boorish and deliberately insulting. It would help us if you could be more specific.'

David gave them a sour smile and took his time. There was no hurry now; it was important that he gave the correct impression. 'Sam deliberately cultivated the image of the ogre. It suited him. It made other people fearful of him and he liked that. Take the people involved in *Herefordshire Horrors.* You'd think Martin Buttivant as Ben Loxton would be in the position to call the shots – no one wants to get rid of the lead in a popular series if it can be avoided. But Sam had some sort of hold over Martin; I don't know exactly what, but Martin still had to watch his step. Sam treated Sandra Rokeby as if she was little better than a high-class prostitute. She's a spirited woman, but she still let Sam get away with things she wouldn't have taken from others. Peg Reynolds is an excellent young actress with a great future, in my opinion. She has both looks and talent and that's a combination which normally pulls a young actress along. She was . . . well, cautious, with Sam Jackson. Probably he knew something about her which the rest of us didn't. He loved to feel he held that sort of advantage.'

'Would you say that he only employed people when he had some sort of hold over them?'

'That might well be so, I suppose. I've never considered that theory before, but it makes sense if you knew Sam Jackson. Even our knight of the realm, Sir Bradley Morton, treated Sam with caution. And Brad doesn't need to defer to many people at this stage of his career. Lechery and flatulence are Brad's hobbies, but he was polite, even deferential, to Sam.'

'Why was that?'

Deeney shrugged elaborately. 'Your guess would be as good as mine, chief superintendent. Perhaps it was simply that Brad wanted more work. He's become rather a caricature of himself as he's got older, so that the parts have dried up. Sam would know all about that; he was a shrewd operator and he knew everything that happened on stage and television – in fact, he loved it when anyone underestimated his knowledge. Even Ernie Clark, his assistant producer, and John Watts, who is an experienced and able director, were careful to take nothing for granted where Sam Jackson was concerned.'

Lambert smiled grimly, watching Bert Hook make notes on this. Then he said, 'Which leaves you, Mr Deeney. What sort of hold did Jackson have on you?'

David had been prepared for this, but the shameless directness of it still shook him a little. 'No particular one. Sam was homophobic, but I'm used to that.' He strove to be absolutely calm, to project the view that Jackson's hostility had been routine and unworrying. 'He was years out of date in his attitude to the gay community. I pitied him rather than resented him.'

'But you won't miss him.'

A raw smile, revealing for a second his real hatred of Jackson. 'The world will be a better place without him. *Herefordshire Horrors* will be concluded much more happily without Sam Jackson around to oversee it. I look forward to further work in the series.'

'It is almost two full days now since you heard of Jackson's death. No doubt you have discussed it with your fellow professionals; it is human nature to do so. Who do you think killed Samuel Jackson?'

David Deeney gave them a smile which was almost patronising. 'I have given the matter much thought, as you suggest. I have really no idea.'

NINE

When David Deeney joined his fellow cast members after speaking to the CID men, he found a strangely febrile atmosphere prevailing. It was another fine day and ideal for location shooting, with high white clouds moving slowly across an intensely blue sky. But David sensed a collective unease amongst both those in front of the cameras and those behind them as they prepared for a good day's filming.

Ernie Clark was here as producer, tactfully easing himself from assistant to main man as the week progressed. He was a much more welcome presence that Sam Jackson had ever been. The cessation of Jackson's random insults and scattergun slurs on cast and director should have much improved the ambience on *Herefordshire Horrors*. Yet Deeney sensed a tension amongst everyone on set which was not going to make for fruitful work.

John Watts had been setting up the first scene for filming, giving his final instructions to those involved as to how they should play off each other in a thoroughly professional ensemble manner. But there was not the fruitful exchange with his cast that he would normally have engendered. Above all, there were not the feeble and apprehensive jokes among his cast and technical supporters which he would have expected to characterize this nervous interval before the important business of the day began.

Watts said to Ernie Clark, 'It's quiet today. Quieter than I would have anticipated.'

'Yes. Why's that, do you think?' Clark had his own thoughts, but he wanted to hear what his director thought: Watts was after all the ringmaster in this strange activity. A successful day might stand or fall by his efforts.

'The buzz of excitement which followed Sam's death seems to have died down. People are watching each other cautiously, wondering who killed Sam.' Watts was watching Ernie Clark, speculating on what he might know, what he might have done, and what might happen next. It was a unique situation for John, directing a cast in these circumstances. There were normally all sorts of insecurities and petty jealousies amongst actors, but wondering who might have killed their larger-than-life producer was a new conundrum for all of them to cope with. They were a temperamental lot, actors, to start with, and who could predict how this extra problem would affect their conduct during today's filming?

Clark said, 'There are a lot of things to sort out. I'm trying to make the transfer of production from Sam to me as smooth as I can, so that the location shooting can proceed with as little interruption as possible.'

He spoke cautiously and formally. John Watts realized that they were fencing with each other, showing a caution in their exchanges which did not normally prevail. It was the situation which was dictating this, not their personalities. He realized with a shock that they were probably both wondering what degree of involvement the other might have in this death which was now hanging over them all. 'Do you think the police know who killed Sam?'

'I don't know. They haven't said much to me. I imagine if they had anything definite, we'd see signs of action from them.' Clark knew the police wanted to speak to him, but the distrust he felt between them prevented him from telling John Watts that.

'Motive, means and opportunity.' Watts smiled grimly. 'Those are things Inspector Ben Loxton is fond of quoting in our fictional series.'

'Lots of us had those. Sam had a capacity for making enemies.'

'You had the greatest motive, I suppose, Ernie. You are the one who gains most in the new situation.' It was out before Watts could prevent it, shocking himself in the bald accusation it carried. He must be more on edge than he'd thought, he supposed.

Clark glanced hard at him, interweaving his powerful fingers and holding his hands firm in his lap, as if he saw that as the only method of keeping them static. 'Thanks for that.' He tried to force a smile and failed. 'I certainly intend to be the biggest gainer. I've put up with Sam Jackson and his villainies for years, at closer quarters than anyone else. Perhaps I've earned myself some reward.'

John Watts tried to retrieve the gaffe he felt he'd just made. 'That will benefit the company at large. I've already pointed that out to them.' He hadn't, but he told himself now that he would do so as soon as the opportunity arose. 'I presume the series will go ahead, with further episodes to follow *Herefordshire Horrors*.'

'I don't see why not. We're generating enough profits from around the world to finance future series for as long as the public wants them.'

'Regular members of the cast will be glad to hear that,' said John.

'And its regular director, I hope,' said Clark evenly.

Watts grinned wryly. 'It's a money-spinner for all of us. It won't make us into cultural icons, but not many of us are in a position to be scornful about Inspector Loxton and his adventures. He's our bread and butter.'

It was at that point that Detective Inspector Christopher Rushton appeared, exactly on cue, it seemed to Watts. 'Mr Clark? Chief Superintendent Lambert and Detective Sergeant Hook would like a few minutes with you, as soon as possible, sir.'

'You haven't been on site much since you spoke briefly with us on Wednesday.' Lambert made it sound like an accusation.

Ernie Clark wasn't a man to back off. You didn't work as Sam Jackson's deputy for seven years without learning to look out for yourself. 'There's been a lot to do, after Sam's unforeseen death. What's going on here and in the studios demands a budget of millions of pounds. I'm now the one who's responsible for seeing the funds are available to keep all this going.'

'It's quite a responsibility.'

'Yes it is. I've no doubt *Herefordshire Horrors* will be successful, as previous episodes have been. To make sure that the future is equally prosperous demands a lot of work behind the scenes.'

'Which is what has occupied you since Jackson died. However, we do need to speak to you.'

'You haven't yet established who killed Sam?' Ernie tried not to sound too truculent. He should after all be willing them on to arrest the murderer of his former colleague, whatever Sam's faults. You couldn't condone murder.

Ernie Clark was squat and powerful physically and he looked very sure of himself. Remarkably self-satisfied, thought the detective duo who now confronted him. He couldn't help his appearance, perhaps, but it would be more seemly if he looked upset. Lambert said acidly, 'I have no doubt you have been busy, Mr Clark. You are also one of the biggest gainers from this death.'

An answering smile, telling them that he felt in control of this situation. 'My colleague John Watts has just pointed out to me that I had motive, means and opportunity for Sam's killing. I hope you are not about to arrest me because of that.'

Lambert scarcely bothered to smile in response. He said wearily, 'Other people have those things too, though you may be the most obvious possessor. The law dictates that we must have more solid evidence before we consider an arrest. Did you visit Mr Jackson in his caravan on the morning of his death?'

'I spent a little time with Sam, yes. He wanted to know how the location shooting was going and whether we would need an extension to the time we'd already agreed. Location work is the most expensive part of this whole enterprise. Sam was always keen on keeping it as short and efficient as possible.' He spoke slowly, rather as if he was explaining himself to intelligent but ill-informed children.

'But you argued with him?'

He wondered if others had heard the sound of their raised voices and reported it. You could never be certain how much the police knew, what had been reported to them by others in the last day or so. There were probably mischievous tongues at work here. Actors were good at gossip and often malevolent with it, in his experience. 'It was an argument Sam and I had with each episode. You can't shoot everything in a studio without losing authenticity. Sam knew that, but he had to go through his ritual of protest each time, as though only he understood the realities of finance and what it cost to shoot in places like this.'

'That must have been tiresome for you.'

'It was one of the recurrent labours of the assistant producer. That and the day-to-day dogsbody work of making sure everything necessary was here on site and ready to go, so that no time was wasted. That's where my real work is done. That's where serious money is wasted if I am less than efficient and everything isn't ready for John Watts and his cast to move and for the cameras to roll.'

'What time did you last see Jackson?'

'I can't be precise. Some time just before noon, I think.'

'Did you notice anything unusual in his demeanour then? Any sort of apprehension, for instance?'

'No. He was his normal ebullient self.' Ernie had chosen that word carefully before he came here. He had decided it was better than 'truculent' or 'quarrelsome' when you were speaking of a dead man. 'Pugnacious' might have been acceptable, he supposed – Sam had always been that.

'And you left him in good health and cheerful?'

'As cheerful as he ever was. Sam didn't think it was good tactics to show cheerfulness: he thought other people might think he was relaxing.'

'So who do you think went in there and killed him, Mr Clark?'

He smiled at them, showing them he wasn't shocked by the question, showing that they weren't going to throw him off balance with their aggressive approach. 'I've given that plenty of thought in the last couple of days. I've come up with lots of candidates, but no certainty. As I haven't got what you referred to just now as evidence, I can't offer you any realistic suggestions.'

'Even speculation might be useful to us at this stage.'

Clark smiled, folding his arms across his broad chest. 'It wouldn't be informed speculation, so it wouldn't be fair or useful to offer it.'

Lambert didn't press him, sensing that this man would give them no less and no more than he had determined to do. 'As we said, you appear to be the man who has gained most by this, whether or not you had any connection with it or knowledge of it. If you are innocent, it is very much in your interest that we make an early arrest. It is also your civic duty to offer us any help you can in this matter. I look forward to hearing more from you in due course.'

Bert Hook had said nothing throughout these brisk exchanges between his chief and Clark. Instead, he had carefully watched the man who was now the sole producer of the Inspector Loxton series and made the occasional note. He looked hard at Lambert once the man had left the murder room, sensing some of John's frustration at the cool control of the man who now ran everything which was being busily enacted around them. 'He's a cool one, that. I don't think he said anything here that he hadn't rehearsed beforehand.'

Lambert smiled his frustration. 'They're a strange lot all round here, Bert. I find them so, anyway. They're used to deceiving people. It's their trade, and it's been so for so long that they now seem to find it difficult to distinguish between fact and fiction. I get the impression with some of them that if they can sell us a falsehood, that will give them more pleasure and professional satisfaction than telling us the truth.'

Bert grinned. 'It's probably the artistic temperament. It tends to produce lying bastards.'

'Is that how you'd describe the man we've just seen?'

'I'm not sure. He's not an actor, remember. He's more of an entrepreneur. A businessman among these artists, who attends to the practicalities.'

'Even more likely to be a lying bastard, then.'

'No comment, sir. But he is the one who's gained most by Jackson's death, and he seems inordinately pleased with himself about that.'

'He's got plenty of nerve, certainly. If he's the one who put paid to Jackson, he'll have planned it thoroughly and covered his tracks effectively.'

The man who was the subject of this judgement would have been flattered by the verdict on his competence. Ernie Clark drove away from the location site now, feeling the accusations and the intrigue slipping away behind him as he went. They'd seen his competence, because he had been content to display that to them. He was even a little vain about it; but he knew that he must be careful not to seem over-confident and glib about what had happened and what it was going to mean for him.

He wondered what the actors were making of Sam's death. He could imagine the frenzied discussions in the hotel since the death had been discovered on Tuesday. There would have been all sorts of speculation, some of it wildly wide of the mark, some of it more reasonable. They had a talent for melodrama, the acting profession. They preferred the bizarre solution to the obvious one – not that there was anything obvious about this, of course.

Part of him wished that he'd been able to listen to some of the wilder speculations. There would be conspiracy theories, in due course, if the police did not come up with a speedy arrest. Perhaps even if they did – conspiracy theorists and wildly imaginative actors never let an arrest and an obvious solution get in the way of an interesting theory. But he knew that he was better away from that hotbed of gossip and accusations. He was staying in his own house on the outskirts of Gloucester and pleasantly isolated from the furore following Jackson's death.

Sam had stayed here with him on the night before his death, when he was newly arrived in the area for the location shooting. The police had been here, of course, on the night after Sam's death. They had removed the clothes from his room, even taken away the sheets and the bedding for forensic examination, assuring Mr Clark earnestly that they would be returned in due course if they produced nothing significant.

They would have been interested in a loaded revolver, for certain. But that had been locked away before they investigated the rather sterile guest room where Sam Jackson had spent his last night on this earth. Ernie opened the locked drawer in his desk and examined it now. A small and innocent-looking thing, for something with so lethal a potential. The metal gleamed softly around the very visible maker's name: Beretta. A well-known name, he thought, though he was no expert on firearms. It occurred to him for the first time that it would have suited Sam Jackson's image to carry a pistol. Sam would have enjoyed giving people the impression that he might need to defend himself at any moment from the multitude of enemies he had amassed in the world. But he never had, as far as Ernie was aware.

He could have done with having a weapon like this with him on the one occasion when he had needed it, when his innocent necktie had been enough to see the life choked out of him on Tuesday. Ernie Clark took the pistol from the drawer and put it in his pocket as he went out to his car. You couldn't be too careful, with a murderer still not apprehended by the police.

Back on the location site near Oldford, Chief Superintendent Lambert was interviewing the final major histrionic suspect. Perhaps he had unconsciously chosen to put Sir Bradley Morton last, since the theatrical knight was almost an amalgam of the traits which disturbed John Lambert about actors as interviewees.

Morton arrived as if this were yet another opportunity for him to display his skills and knowledge, though being a murder suspect must surely be a unique occurrence even in his vast range of life experiences. 'It's taken you a long time to get round to me,' he said accusingly, as if it were a dereliction of CID duty to put him anywhere but at the top of the investigational list.

'We issued an important initial instruction,' said Lambert. 'We said that anyone with significant knowledge to contribute should come to us immediately, without waiting for a formal interview. Are you now telling us that you are in possession of such knowledge?'

Morton considered the matter carefully before deciding that the only safe policy was to proclaim his ignorance. 'I'm afraid I have no significant piece of evidence to volunteer,' he boomed sonorously. 'I have an intimate knowledge of the theatrical world and its many idiosyncrasies, which I am ready and willing to put at your disposal.'

'I'm sure we shall be grateful for that,' said Lambert, with an irony which was lost on the larger-than-life theatrical presence sitting before him.

Sir Bradley inspected the upright chair they had set ready for him and disposed himself upon it so that it looked somehow like an armchair, from which he now held forth to these lesser mortals who were presuming to question him. He had on a bow tie and a lemon yellow shirt beneath a green cardigan. He carried them as though they were expensive robes of state and he was playing a Shakespearean king. He said, 'I hope you are making progress in this matter. Sam Jackson was a dear friend of mine.'

'Was he, indeed? Well, that's good to hear. I think the other people we've spoken to have declared without exception that they did not like him. Perhaps a friend of his will be able to offer us a different perspective on this, DS Hook.'

'That would be most useful, sir.'

'We were not intimates, Chief Superintendent Lambert.' Sir Bradley was booming again; his tones seemed to bounce off the insensitive walls of the murder room and demand a loftier hall.

Lambert forced a smile. 'I'll be frank with you, Sir Bradley. As I say, most people have declared a dislike, even a loathing, of Samuel Jackson. They put up with him because they had to. He had the power and the money to control their future fortunes. They did not like that, but they recognized the reality of the situation.'

Morton smiled the broadest and most understanding of his many smiles. 'I do not condemn them. I understand them. They are not all as fortunate as I am. When one has reached a certain eminence in this profession, one can afford to be more cavalier about these things. I am not short of offers of work – indeed, I find that these days I have to make a careful choice amongst the many opportunities available to me. I recognize that I am fortunate in this, but I flatter myself that I have earned a certain standing over the years. This is an uncertain profession, especially for young people starting out in it, but when you reach my advanced years and have a record of successes behind you, you are able to treat theatrical and television producers with a degree of condescension.'

Lambert was thoroughly irritated by the man's evasions. He raised his eyebrows elaborately. 'Really? We must have been misinformed. Some people have suggested that your chances of further work in this series would be enhanced now that Samuel Jackson is no longer around.'

'I don't know who could have told you that. I detect a distaff hand in this. The fair sex are anything but fair, when they have an axe to grind. I'm sure you have found that, in the course of your many successful investigations of serious crime. Whoever is your informant, he or she is much mistaken. Sam and I went back a long way. I was a well-established actor when he was making his way in the business. I offered him a helping hand and in the course of time he was truly grateful. He was virtually begging me to accept an extended role in the Inspector Loxton series when someone removed him from this earth.' It was an extravagant claim, but Brad couldn't see how anyone could refute it, without Jackson around.

'I see, sir. That is most interesting; it is a pity that we were misinformed.'

'Perhaps not exactly misinformed. But I try to take a broad view of life. I may have been biased in Jackson's favour because he put up money to support the man who I think of as our greatest television playwright before he had become a household name.' Brad looked at his listeners and saw only confusion. 'I refer, of course, to my fellow Forest of Dean man, Dennis Potter.' Morton bowed his head reverently. It seemed safe in this context to claim a more intimate relationship with the great man than he had actually enjoyed. 'Dennis grew up in Berry Hill, a Forest of Dean village within twenty miles of here. We had a certain rapport. I recognized his talent early and was pleased to appear in some of his early plays.' Potter might not have remembered that, but he hadn't been around for twenty years and more, so he wasn't going to dispute it. He was one of the links with high culture which Sir Bradley had grown used to claiming for himself.

Lambert studied him closely throughout this, then nodded it away as an irrelevance. 'From what you tell us, you must be very upset by this death, unlike the other people we have spoken to. None of them liked Samuel Jackson. You seem to be the only one who has lost a friend.'

Morton knew that he had shown no more sorrow than anyone else in their hotel. Rather the reverse, in fact. He'd ordered two bottles of claret and made Tuesday night something of a celebration in the dining room. He wondered if that had got back to this shrewd, observant fellow with the lined face and the unblinking grey eyes. 'If you reach my age, you get used to losing friends.' He spoke like a mournful ninety-year-old. Lambert knew from Rushton's notes that Sir Bradley was in fact seventy-three. 'One tries to be philosophical when another one departs. And I suppose Sam Jackson was an old acquaintance rather than an old friend. He was a facilitator; they are important to us, but Sam was not himself of the acting fraternity.'

'But it may well be one of the acting fraternity who killed him, Sir Bradley. Was it you?'

He recoiled as if he had been physically struck. Theatrical, Bert Hook would have called it, had it been an amateur who struck the pose. The knight looked as if he was wondering just how much umbrage he might take at this suggestion. Then he smiled broadly, indicating what a tolerant man he was, despite the honours thrust upon him. 'I suppose you have to ask these things, Mr Lambert, in your role as super-sleuth. These labels accorded to one by the popular press can be tiresome, as you and I both know. I tell you here and now that I did not kill Sam. I did not visit him in his caravan in the hours before his death, which I heartily lament. I trust that my word is good enough for you. I have a certain standing in my profession.'

'And I have worked hard to acquire one in mine, Sir Bradley. Among the things I have learned is to look for facts rather than mere assertions, whoever is involved. When I entered CID many years ago, my inspector gave me three pointers. Assume nothing. Believe no one. Check everything. I have found it good advice over the years.'

'You are a cynic, chief superintendent.'

'Criminals make you that, Sir Bradley. Cynicism becomes part of your professional equipment. Have you any views on who might have killed your friend and facilitator, Samuel Jackson?'

'No. Ernie Clark has gained most by it. But that's probably a cynical observation.'

'It is a fact we have to bear in mind, Sir Bradley. But other people have gained as well. No one except you has lamented this death. Please keep your eyes and your ears open in the days to come. As a Titan of your profession and a highly experienced man, you may well pick up things which other people miss.'

Morton accepted this as a compliment; he met very little irony nowadays and he had long since become accustomed to accepting flattery at face value. He left with a slight bow and what was almost a knightly flourish of his right arm.

Lambert looked at the door for a long moment after he had left. 'What did you make of that?' he asked Hook.

'I think he half-believes the image he has created for himself. I think that like many of his craft he is not good at distinguishing where fantasy ends and the real world begins.'

Lambert looked at his extensive file on Sir Bradley Morton's background. 'Despite what he says, I think he hated our murder victim as much as anyone. I wonder if he did anything about that.'

TEN

The evening was a poet's idyll, calm and mild. The sun stretched unbroken over hill and valley, river and forest, until it sank slowly behind the Welsh mountains, as if reluctant to leave behind this peaceful scene.

The cast and director of *Herefordshire Horrors* congratulated themselves again on the accommodation which had been secured for them. The food and the rooms were excellent here; the hotel had made every effort to anticipate their every need. Whatever their status might be now, all theatricals had lived in the humblest of digs and eaten the humblest of food in their younger days. In Sir Bradley Morton's memorable phrase, they all remembered the days of peeing in sinks at the local rep. Many of the younger cast members had in fact never known rep, but they all knew well what it was to live from hand to mouth and to husband every penny against the uncertainties of their theatrical futures.

This pleasant hotel on the bank of the River Wye was one of the perks of a successful television series, and those who had known much harder times were very happy to take advantage of it. It was May now. Gloucestershire and Herefordshire were enjoying a late-spring heat wave, with temperatures soaring into the mid-twenties and the weather set fair for the next few days. The heavy rain at the beginning of the week had passed away now, and the Wye ran softly in its channel sixty feet below the quiet road.

Actors and director, cameramen, wardrobe mistresses and continuity girls, wandered after dinner along the banks of the Wye, in liaisons which were innocent or exciting, according to choice. The balmy evening and the idyllic setting encouraged romantic notions, as tend to take over when people are away from home and operating in strange and wonderful surroundings. The scent of freshly washed female hair, mingling with the scents of trees and the sound of unseen water, is a heady mix in the warm darkness.

Couples strolled ever more slowly as they completed the return journey to the hotel. Of course, one walks more slowly with an arm round a partner's waist. Some couples separated reluctantly when they reached the entrance to the hotel, with kisses that lingered and were often repeated as a farewell to nature's magical epilogue to the day. Others stayed together, or separated with muttered arrangements to rejoin each other discreetly in the rooms on the upper storeys of the building, where intimacies might be resumed and developed.

Most of this sporadic procession of lovers and opportunists passed beside the car park, which accommodated rows of vehicles parked there for the night. There was some expensive machinery here, but the people enjoying the privacy of the summer darkness had other and more vital concerns than motor transport. No one gave a glance or a thought to the vehicles which sat silently in the spacious parking area behind the hotel.

The dark red Jaguar which was furthest from the walls of the hotel was one of the more impressive vehicles, sleek and low in the darkness, the dew on its roof reflecting the starlight and eventually the crescent moon for anyone who cared to watch. But no one did. The long, low car kept its secret through the night.

It was one of the staff arriving to do the early breakfast shift who found the secret of the Jaguar. The corpse was clearly visible in the sharp morning light. It carried still a startled look, though it had been dead now for many hours. The young woman who found it took a little while to register just what it was. Then her scream rang loud and strong through the morning air.

ELEVEN

It was just after six thirty when the corpse in the Jaguar was discovered. By eight o'clock, a full scene of crime team had been assembled and was about to begin work in the fenced-off section of the car park. John Lambert had been informed of this new death by seven thirty and by eight thirty he was on the spot with Detective Sergeant Hook.

The pathologist had completed his examination of the corpse, or as much as he was able to do of it *in situ*, as the duo arrived. 'Straightforward, from my point of view,' he said. 'Probably not so straightforward from yours.' He tried not to sound too satisfied about that. Dr Patterson gained a secret satisfaction from being involved in lurid deaths, and this seemed certain to be one of those. Almost certainly a second murder in a week, and the police to all appearances baffled – the pathologist thought it fair to use that favourite tabloid word.

Murder has a ghoulish glamour, even for someone as familiar with death as a pathologist. This was different from, and far more intriguing than, the routine road deaths and suicides to which he was more usually called to render his professional services and opinions. Other deaths were simply part of the job, regrettable but routine. Murder had a *Grande Guignole* quality, even for the professionals involved in it. You didn't admit that, of course, especially when you were a balding and experienced man of fifty-three, but you felt an excitement nevertheless.

'He died from a single bullet to the temple, probably nine millimetre calibre. Almost certainly it is still lodged within the skull, since there is no sign of an exit wound. I'll have him on the table and complete my examination before the day's over. You should have my full findings by this evening. Crimes like this one take precedence.'

'You're certain it was murder?'

'As certain as I can be, at this stage. I wouldn't go into court with what we have here, but I'm giving you my firm opinion. It's what you always ask me for.'

Lambert smiled grimly as he gave a tiny nod. 'Tell me why it's murder, Dr Patterson.'

'Principally because there's no sign of a weapon. A single, efficient bullet through the head from no more than three inches and then the weapon is taken away, by person or persons unknown. It's my guess that you'll never see it again.'

'Could this be a professional killer? A hired hit man?'

'More your field than mine, Lambert, but I'd say yes. It has the hallmarks. Efficient, anonymous, almost clinical. And in the sort of isolated place with a notable absence of witnesses which a professional killer might choose. Are there people among your suspects who might have the opportunity and the funds to employ someone like that?'

Lambert sighed. 'I expect so. There are more and more hit men around and more and more people willing and able to employ them.' The police and the law hated professional hit men, because they were the most efficient as well as the most ruthless of killers. Experience told, in this as in other fields. Practice made, if not perfect, highly efficient. And hit men were unemotional, demanding a large fee for their services but not usually acquainted with their victims, which meant they were unaffected by the love, anger or hate which characterized so many killings and provided clues as to their motivation.

Bert Hook said, 'We didn't think the murder of Sam Jackson involved a hit man; a professional killer would have chosen a different time and a different place – somewhere far less public and more anonymous than his caravan on a location film site. Are we saying that this killing is by a different person? It's stretching credulity to say these two deaths aren't connected.'

Lambert grinned at the pathologist. 'Bert is my voice of sanity. He tries to counteract the natural pessimism which goes with the rank of chief superintendent. He's refused the chance to become a detective inspector at least three times; I think he feels it might compromise his natural optimism and sunny outlook on life.'

The pathologist looked doubtfully at the stolid Bert Hook. Like others before him, he was confused by the occasional ironies of this unlikely double act. 'I must be on my way. I wish you well on this one. The press boys will be here shortly to make a meal of it.'

'And of us, no doubt, if we allow it,' said Lambert. 'Can you give us a time of death?'

'Almost certainly last night rather than this morning, from the temperatures I've recorded. If you can check when this fellow last ate, my analysis of stomach contents later today will give you a reasonably accurate idea of when he died. Meantime, I hope the car provides you with some significant clue as to who might have done this. The angle of the wound and everything about the position of the corpse indicates that he was shot from the front passenger seat.'

John Lambert watched the SOC team dusting door handles inside and out for fingerprints. 'The young woman who raised the alarm this morning opened the driver's door,' said the head of the team with a shake of the head, as if deploring the lack of professionalism he met so often in the public.

'Good job she investigated. The poor sod might still be sitting here waiting to be discovered if she'd been as determined to mind her own business as so many people are nowadays.' Lambert looked at the driving keys, which had already been dusted. 'Were those left in the ignition overnight?'

'Yes. Well, I presume so. They were here when we arrived.'

'Probably not a hit man, then. He'd almost certainly have locked the car and taken the keys away – anything to delay discovery and make our job a little harder. Have you found anything which might be significant yet?' The SOC officer was a civilian but an ex-policeman, who knew exactly the sort of detail which might be significant for CID.

'We've bagged hairs and clothes fibres from floor and seats. But most of them probably pre-date last night. This is a nice motor, but it's quite a while since the interior was cleaned.'

'And we'll probably need an arrest before we can match up your trophies. We're in no position to demand a DNA sample from everyone staying in the hotel who might have a connection with this.'

Lambert looked sourly, even resentfully, at the body of Ernie Clark, as if it was the victim's fault that he couldn't provide them with better guidance as to his killer.

The news of the body in the car park had been broken to the cast and ancillary staff of *Hertfordshire Horrors* at breakfast, which was around eight o'clock for most of them. The tradition of theatricals rising late after long nights in the theatre and hours of unwinding before retiring to bed late in the night dated from a situation which was now rare rather than characteristic. When you were involved in location shooting for a television series, you had to be on the site early; you caused highly expensive delays if you were not and were likely to find yourself redundant at the end of your present contract.

John Watts heard about the death at twelve minutes past eight. By twenty past eight, he had been down to the end of the car park and found the scene of the crime already fenced off from public access. But he had confirmed that the victim of this latest outrage was in fact Ernest Clark. By just after nine o'clock, he was completing his third phone call stemming from this knowledge. 'I'm not scrambling for funds, Mr Armitage. I'm offering to let you in on a good thing. Yes, I'm demanding complete control, but I'm suggesting to you that that is the most efficient method of securing a proper return on your investment. I know exactly what is going on in this series. I have directed every episode since the outset and I know what is planned for the future. I'm demanding complete control because that is the most efficient way forward for everyone – for the new investors we shall need as well as for everyone who will remain involved in the Inspector Loxton series.'

Watts put down the phone and smiled. Armitage was interested – more than interested. Once you stripped away the financial-speak of the theatrical investor, he was positively eager. He'd be stupid not to be. The Ben Loxton series was the nearest thing to a guaranteed financial return you could be offered in the uncertain worlds of theatre and television. Armitage would be in, if he had the money available, and so would the others he'd rung before him. And he'd make sure there was a strong holding for himself in whatever scheme was eventually adopted. He'd pour in every pound he had and he'd up his own salary as director. You had to look after number one in this game. Not everyone was as adept at that as John Watts. Theatrical tycoon as well as respected director, the show business pages would be saying by the end of the year. You had to take advantages of opportunities when they offered themselves, whether unexpected or otherwise.

The anonymous grey van which the police knew as the 'meat wagon' was preparing to remove the body of Ernest Clark from the Jaguar which had given him much pleasure before becoming the scene of his death. The photographer was crouched at a very strange angle in the car, taking a last picture of the body and where it was slumped. All of this would probably prove irrelevant, but you never knew in advance what pictures or what samples might become vital supporting evidence in a court of law. The job of a scene of crime team was to cover all possible options with the evidence from the spot which might support them.

The Jaguar was at the very end of the car park, whence it would shortly be removed for intensive forensic examination in the police laboratories. Lambert and Hook walked out to the road beside it and looked down at the Wye, running low and peaceful past this spot where a man had died so violently. Lambert said suddenly and unexpectedly, 'Simon James is a fly fisherman, isn't he?'

Hook was surprised. Simon James was a sergeant, but he was uniform, not CID. Bert didn't think the chief would even have registered his name, so preoccupied was he with serious crimes like the present one in his final detective years. But John Lambert registered all sorts of information and he rarely forgot a name. Bert said, 'He's very keen, is Simon. I fished with him a couple of times myself, before you made me take up golf. But I was never in his class. He fishes this area of the river – right down to Ross-on-Wye, I think.'

'He'll probably know this stretch well. There are a couple of very inviting pools just north and south of here. It's a long shot, but I'd like him to come out here with a single police frogman and take a quick look for the weapon which killed Ernest Clark. They should confine themselves to a hundred yards north and south of here. It doesn't merit any more resources, because it's such an outside chance, but there isn't that much deep water on this stretch.'

'You think the killer might have flung away his murder weapon so close to the scene of the crime?'

'I'd want to get rid of it as soon as I could, if I'd just shot someone. If I was driving away, I might look for a foolproof spot miles away from here, but my present guess is that it was someone staying in the hotel who did this. I'd have wanted to be rid of an incriminating firearm as quickly as possible. It's worth a try, that's all. I'm hoping Simon James has expert knowledge of this stretch, which might help him to pinpoint the search.'

Bert Hook phoned the station and spoke to Sergeant James himself. That solid officer was surprised, but only for a moment. The idea of directing a police frogman obviously appealed to Simon James. He'd be up here by early evening, he hoped, when he'd recruited a frogman who was a fellow angler and knew this stretch of the Wye almost as well as he did. At the very latest by tomorrow morning, which was Saturday. Any surprise had left his voice by now. The ways of detective chief superintendents were strange indeed, and largely a closed book to Station Sergeant James.

DS Hook reckoned as they walked back to the hotel that John Lambert must be feeling more than usually baffled by this second death. Neither of them knew that at that very moment, a police search of Ernie Clark's house was revealing information which would prove significant in this baffling pair of murders.

Lambert decided that they would continue to use the murder room they had already set up at the location site for this second murder also. It would enable the expensive location filming which was such a matter of concern to the crew to continue whilst the detective team studied any significant or suspicious actions on the part of those involved.

Before their first interview, DI Chris Rushton brought in

information he had taken in a phone call from the detective sergeant and team who had searched the small house occupied by Ernie Clark on the outskirts of Gloucester. 'I'm about to put this on the files I've compiled on the people concerned, sir. I thought you might like to have the gist of it as quickly as possible.'

Lambert nodded his thanks. He had scarcely time to register the first significant facts before David Deeney knocked quietly at the door and came into the murder room. He sat in the chair set ready for him and said, 'Bad business, this. None of us liked Sam Jackson, as you've no doubt gathered by now, but Ernie Clark was a different sort of man. He didn't go out of his way to offend you for no reason other than an innate nastiness, as Sam did.'

He was nervous, tumbling out words to fill the silence he felt was threatening him. That was unusual among these actors, who seemed experts in deception, even when they had nothing really important to hide. John Lambert found the man's anxiety curiously reassuring and normal, so that when Deeney finally came to a halt he let the silence stretch for a moment. Then he asked quietly, 'Did you arrange to meet Mr Clark in the hotel car park last night?'

'No, of course I didn't.'

'There's no "of course" about it, as far as we are concerned, Mr Deeney. Mr Clark wasn't staying at your hotel, but at his home in Gloucester. It seems almost certain that someone arranged a meeting with him last night. Not in the hotel, because they would have been seen there and no one has reported a sighting. A secret meeting, then, at the point of the car park furthest from the hotel. That's where the car and Mr Clark's body were discovered this morning.'

'And the person who arranged this meeting is the person who killed Ernie?'

'That seems at the moment highly probable, as I'm sure you'd agree. Is there anyone available to support your story that it wasn't you who asked him to come?'

'No. It's difficult to prove a negative. You must be able to see that.'

'Difficult but not impossible. If you were with someone else for most of the evening, for instance, that would be helpful to you and to us. Or if a member of the hotel staff could confirm that you were in one of the bars or even in your room for most of the evening, we would be delighted to record that. We haven't yet been able to pinpoint a time of death, but we may be able to do that in the next few hours.'

'I was alone in my room for most of the evening. I do not have a witness to that.'

Bert Hook made a note of this, then looked up into the anxious brown eyes beneath the carefully parted black hair. 'Why are you staying in the hotel, Mr Deeney?'

'What do you mean? We're all staying there. All the cast and many of the support staff.'

'Ernie Clark wasn't staying with you. Someone had to get him to come here so that they could kill him.'

'Ernie had his own house in Gloucester. It was natural that he should stay there. He had Sam Jackson staying there with him until someone decided to kill Sam on Tuesday.'

'Just as you have your own house in Oxford. Most of the cast are London-based and need accommodation here, but your house is scarcely more than an hour's drive from here. I'm surprised you didn't elect to stay with your partner there and travel each day for the location filming.'

David was uncomfortable. He stared at Hook's weather-beaten, unmenacing face as if he could scarcely believe his embarrassment stemmed from this source. 'It's not easy getting out of Oxford in the mornings. The rush hour's a nightmare.'

'But much easier journeying out than journeying in. And you didn't have to be on this site at the crack of dawn. On only one of the days this week were you scheduled to be shooting the first scene here.'

'Why this sudden interest in my domestic arrangements, DS Hook?'

A bland smile from the bland face. 'We become interested in all sorts of apparently inconsequential things when there is a murder, sir. Had you been at home in Oxford last night rather than installed in the hotel by the River Wye, you would have been in no position to arrange a meeting there with a murder victim.'

David Deeney looked hard at him for a moment, then said, 'There's another reason for staying in the hotel with the rest of the cast. An actor's reason. Probably one you wouldn't understand.'

'Try me, Mr Deeney.' There was no trace of a smile in Hook's amiable features.

'Team spirit. When you're part of an ongoing series where many people appear in successive episodes, you become a team and have the advantages of a team. We call it ensemble playing. It's not that we all become bosom pals, but if you keep together as a cast you gain certain indefinable advantages.'

'Indefinable?'

How absolute the knave was! It was almost as if he was having fun, but there was still no trace of a smile on the dutiful, unchanging face. David had a sudden inspiration. 'You've played cricket at a high level, I believe, Detective Sergeant Hook. You must be aware how the general performance lifts when you have the team ethic operating.'

'Indeed, yes. But clustering round the bat and catching everything doesn't seem quite the same as acting a scene on stage or film.'

'Not quite the same, but with similar elements. You help each other and set up effects for each other, when you're used to playing scenes together. You get to know each other's idiosyncrasies as actors. Ensemble playing lifts a scene and gives it things it wouldn't have if we were all strangers to each other.'

'And you feel the ensemble effect is enhanced by your staying in the hotel rather than being at home with your partner.' Hook nodded slowly, making this sound the unlikeliest of reasons for Deeney to be in the hotel where murder had been planned and delivered. 'You feel you know your fellow actors involved in *Herefordshire Horrors* quite intimately, then?'

David said with what dignity he could muster, 'I know them a little better than if I had gone home to Oxford each night rather than staying with them in Herefordshire. I hope that might lead to a tiny improvement in what we produce collectively. That is all I'm claiming.'

Bert Hook, who knew all about ensemble playing and admired it when he saw it in the theatre, looked suitably dubious. 'I understand, sir. But you found on Wednesday, the day after our first murder, that you had something sufficiently pressing to take you on a flying visit to Oxford. In the middle of the day, between two different scenes you were filming on the location site here. The strength of the ensemble does not seem to have been your priority on Wednesday.'

David was shaken by the detail they knew about his movements. Perhaps that was why they allotted such huge teams to murder enquiries. He said as lightly as he could, 'You're making more of this than is warranted. I simply found that the shooting schedules on Wednesday left me with three hours to myself in the middle of the day. I thought it would be a good opportunity to zip home and see my partner, Trevor Fisher. It was an impulse after my first scene had gone well, There was no more to it than that.'

'One of our officers spoke to Mr Fisher yesterday. It's standard procedure to check with partners, when we're checking the movements of people involved in murder investigations.'

David would like to have claimed that he knew all about that. Instead, he said dully, 'I didn't have my phone on last night. I expect Trevor tried to tell me he'd been questioned.'

'Perhaps he did. He certainly gave our officer one interesting piece of information. He was puzzled by the fact that you chose on that flying visit to dispose of a perfectly good pair of trainers.'

David's heart leapt within his breast, so violently that he felt for an absurd moment that the movement might have been visible. 'They were well worn. They'd had their day. I'd been meaning to get rid of them for a while. I saw the refuse lorry approaching our house as I turned into the street. I think that is what prompted the action.'

'Scarcely worn, Mr Fisher said. He even considered whether he might retrieve them for you, but found that he was just too late to save them.'

Bloody Trevor! Sometimes he was so damned innocent that he didn't think anyone else could have anything to hide. Childlike, he was, at times. But David knew even through his annoyance that it was this bright innocence which had been one of Trevor's attractions for him when they made their first tentative moves towards each other. Innocence was something you didn't meet too often in the acting profession. He found it refreshing to get away from the petty jealousies and insecurities of his daytime occupation to the private intimacies of his life with honest Trevor Fisher.

There was no easy lie to free him from this, nothing which would convince that round, interrogative face of Hook's which was suddenly so challenging. David Deeney stared down at the shabby floor of the murder room as he said, 'I panicked, I suppose. I'd been to see Sam Jackson in his caravan on the morning when he died. I'd walked through mud to get there. I knew I must have left some sort of deposit from the soles of my trainers in there. I thought you'd pick that up and identify it as coming from my shoes and think that if I'd been there I must have killed Jackson. It suddenly became very important to me to get rid of those trainers. I didn't even know that Trevor knew I'd slipped them in the rubbish.'

'Did you twist Samuel Jackson's tie around his neck before you left his caravan on Tuesday?'

'No. He was in good health when I left him.'

Hook nodded as if this reply was exactly what he had anticipated. 'Why did you visit Jackson at that time, Mr Deeney?'

'I wanted some guarantee of more employment in the future. I felt that my work in this particular episode, *Herefordshire Horrors*, was pretty good; you get to know with experience when things have gone well. I felt that John Watts as director would support that view. I thought it might be the right moment for me to build a little more security into my future.'

'Were you successful?'

'No. I should have known my man better, shouldn't I? Sam said he didn't give any guarantees to filthy pooftahs, that he would employ straight men if the opportunity presented itself.' He was staring at the floor again, feeling the hopelessness of life and of his present situation. 'He was very old-fashioned in his attitudes, was Sam Jackson. I should never have thought I could change that.'

They waited until he reluctantly raised his eyes before

commenting on this. Then Lambert said, 'Is there anyone who can confirm this for us?'

'No. I wasn't anxious to proclaim to the others that I was touting for work.'

'Then please don't leave the area without keeping us informed of your movements.'

TWELVE

Peg Reynolds was still in the hotel after the rest of the cast of *Herefordshire Horrors* had left. She knew that she wouldn't be required for shooting until late morning.

She snatched an early coffee in the lounge, wishing that she was less noticeable than she seemed to be. She wanted to blend into the background, to be as unremarked as any piece of furniture in this conventionally furnished room. But waiters and cleaners seemed to notice her, however much she pretended to be immersed in the newspaper she was trying to make herself read. The truth was that with her youth, her large brown eyes, her shimmering black hair and her air of vulnerability, Peg was always going to compel attention, whether she required it or not.

Like many attractive, intelligent, otherwise sensible women, Peg showed bad judgement only in her choice of men. She was becoming aware of this, but was as yet unwilling to admit it even to herself. She didn't want to go back to her room and face James Turner, but she knew she would have to do just that. She lingered over her coffee, hoping to make the exchange as brief as possible, but eventually she had to go. The last thing she wanted was James appearing here and causing a public scene with her, especially with so many police around after last night's events.

James was rifling through the contents of her handbag when she got back to the room. That depressed her, but it didn't really shock her any more; she'd caught him doing it at least twice in the last month. She said dully, 'You won't find anything to interest you in there. There's no money to speak of: you had that long ago.'

'That's right, rub my nose in it! Don't let the fact that I'm out of work and struggling to find it escape me for a moment, will you? Peg Reynolds has work and her partner hasn't! Peg

Reynolds is flavour of the month and is delighted that James Turner isn't. It enables her to patronise him and remind him perpetually what a worthless piece of shit he is!'

His self-loathing grew with every phrase as his voice rose. But that was no use to her; his contempt for himself only made him more violent and less predictable. She spoke carefully, trying to avoid words or phrases which might annoy him. 'I've got to go, James. I need to be there on time for the shooting. We can't afford to lose what I earn.'

'"We can't afford to lose what I earn." So I'll be off now, enjoying being in work, ready to offer a good shag to anyone who can offer me the next job in return.'

She didn't want to rise to the bait; she knew that he was merely lashing out wildly in an attempt to hurt her. But she heard herself saying, 'That isn't true and you know it's not. I've never shagged anyone to get work and I don't intend to start now.'

'Little Miss Muffet wouldn't do anything like that, would she? Little Miss Muffet would keep her arse firmly on her tuffet and tell anyone who came by to go shag himself! The same as she tells me to fuck off and find my own work and stop bothering her.'

He was handsome, she thought, even in this state. His hair looked even more attractive when it was dishevelled than when it was neatly combed; his handsome, regular features were even more compelling when they were flushed, like this. Why couldn't he get acting work when other, less good-looking men seemed to have it offered to them regularly? Perhaps he just wasn't a very good actor. She'd been too close to him even to consider that possibility; she'd thought that like other people who were often 'resting' he was just unlucky in an overcrowded profession. But maybe he just wasn't as good as he thought he was and as she'd unthinkingly accepted that he was. But how could she ever put it to him that perhaps he should consider some other sort of employment? She shivered involuntarily on this warm morning at the very thought of that.

He had her upper arms in his hands now, squeezing hard. The bruises had almost gone, but they'd be back if he lost his rag again. She shut her eyes, knowing that she could not handle him when he was like this, feeling as though the ground was slipping away beneath her feet. 'Please don't do that, James. You know that I bruise easily. Everyone will be asking how I got the marks if they see them.'

He smiled for the first time now, but his lips had no humour in them. 'And everyone will be offering their sympathy to dear little Miss Muffet! Everyone will be asking who the naughty man was and how they might best punish him. By denying him work, of course. Let's all see that James Turner doesn't get any parts offered! Let's all rub it in by making sure that creepy little Peg Reynolds gets even more work thrown at her!'

She felt his hands tightening into that vice-like grip, knew now that the bruises would be back, that she'd be wearing the only summer dress she had with sleeves. But what about her costume for the shoot? Would that be sleeveless? Even short sleeves would show the damage he was doing to her. She struggled, but she knew that she wasn't strong enough, that this would only make the damage worse. She shouted desperately, 'Let go of me, James! I've done everything I could to get you work in the last week. More than you know I've done!'

He let go of her at last and they stood panting fiercely, their faces less than two feet apart. She wondered why she had spoken. James Turner was wondering exactly what she had meant.

One policewoman and several civilians were still working in the ribboned-off section at the end of the car par when Peg Reynolds crept trembling into her battered blue Corsa and drove away to the location site and her work.

Sandra Rokeby looked uncharacteristically nervous as she entered the murder room. The public image which was so important to her was built on confidence, on parading her physical wares and pretending to be much more of a femme fatale than she really was. But she had a feeling that these two experienced CID men saw through her every move. She felt more naked with them than she had felt with anyone for a long time. Since she was last in love perhaps. That was a long time ago. Love made you vulnerable and she couldn't live with vulnerability. Not only her public image but her whole life depended on the brash, humorous, sexual image she had laboured for years to create.

Lambert felt it, and felt it strongly enough to comment on it. He went for vulnerability head-on wherever he saw it and whatever the cause of it, because the odds were against him and he needed to exploit any kind of weakness he discovered. 'You look nervous this morning.'

A wan smile. She'd spent a long time in front of her mirror before she'd left her hotel room, but she'd known there were limits to what she could do with this forty-eight-year-old face and she'd had the sense to respect those limits. If you tried to do too much with make-up on a pale, increasingly lined face it didn't work: you merely looked tarty. There was a big difference between sexy and tarty, of which Sandra was intensely conscious, however much some of her public might confuse them. She'd applied lipstick and eye make-up discreetly, but she knew that she nevertheless looked like a pale and worried woman in her late forties. She said in response to the chief superintendent, 'I've a right to look nervous, Mr Lambert. I've seen two powerful men whom I knew quite well murdered within three days. I wonder who might be next.'

'You're already sure last night's death was murder, then? We haven't yet released any details.'

'Ernie Clark was a fit and healthy man, as far as I know. Far healthier than Sam Jackson, I imagine. In view of what happened to Jackson on Tuesday, it would surprise me if last night's death was anything but murder.'

'Last night? We haven't had the time of death confirmed yet, Miss Rokeby. It seems you know more than we do.'

She gave them a wan smile. 'I saw the girl who found him in the car this morning. Helped to calm her down a little, I hope – she's a nice kid. It was her impression that Ernie died last night. And she spoke of a bullet wound; that would explain why I knew this was murder, wouldn't it?'

She looked at him steadily, responding to his note of aggression, almost welcoming the challenge, it seemed. He said, 'Where were you last night, Miss Rokeby? As I said, we haven't pinpointed a time of death yet, so I'd like you to describe your movements throughout the evening.'

'The evening but not the night? How disappointing, when I could give you a resounding negative. I slept alone last night, you see.'

'And earlier in the evening?'

This was all right. She'd anticipated the question and had her answer ready. But she still needed to be careful with these watchful men, who might or might not know as little as they claimed. 'I ate dinner with the rest of the cast of *Herefordshire Horrors*. Well, most of them.'

It was a deliberate invitation for a question, which was duly delivered. 'Could you tell us who of the cast wasn't with you at dinner?'

'Peg Reynolds.'

'And where was she?'

A slight, experienced smile. 'You'll need to ask her that, won't you? Young blood will have its day, they say, so I can't tell you what she and her boyfriend were up to, though I can make a good guess. They came into the dining room when the rest of us had already been there for about an hour. They sat at their own table and had their own conversation. You can't read anything significant into that. It's what they've done all week.'

Hook made a note and spoke for the first time. 'This boyfriend of Miss Reynolds. A member of our team took a brief statement from him earlier in the week, but he was not on this location site at the time of Mr Jackson's death and so is not suspected of murder. So neither Chief Superintendent Lambert nor I have met him. What sort of man is he?'

It was left very open-ended, as though her extensive knowledge of the other sex would enable her to give a prompt and accurate assessment of the man. Unlike most of her colleagues, she didn't underestimate this quietly spoken sergeant with the village bobby exterior. 'His name is James Turner. I should say that I hardly know him, I suppose, but in the interests of accuracy I shall give you my opinion that he's a nasty piece of work.'

'Nasty in what way?'

'In almost every way, from Peg's point of view. Their affair won't last. The question is, how much damage will it do to Peg Reynolds before she finally sends him on his way?'

'Is he violent?'

She looked hard at Hook, who was about her own age, but suddenly reminded her of the father she had not thought about in years. 'You mean could he have killed Ernie Clark last night, don't you? I expect he could, if the circumstances were right.'

'You'd better tell us what those would be.'

She stopped, looking at the shabby floor, concentrating on what she was going to say, thinking not of the impression of herself she was creating but of what she was going to say about this strange, handsome, sexy, highly dangerous man who had captivated Peg Reynolds. 'James Turner is desperate to get acting work. I've no idea whether he deserves it or not. Merit isn't always the key thing in our profession; luck and who you know are far more important for a youngster. Turner's got looks, which always help. My guess is that with his handsome face and someone like Peg Reynolds on his side he can't be much good if he's out of work. But I could be quite wrong.'

She didn't sound as if she thought that at all likely, Hook thought. 'Miss Reynolds has been trying to help him?'

'She's a good woman, Peg. She's got more talent in her little finger than I had at her age, but I try not to hate her for that. But she's besotted with that bloody man Turner. We're stupid like that, you know, we women. We lose all sense of perspective when someone whispers nice things and gives us a bit of pleasure between the sheets.'

Hook smiled at her flash of bitterness. 'I've known a few men behave stupidly and lose all judgement when similarly affected by women. And not all of them were young men. They seem to take longer to grow out of it than women.'

She looked hard at him for a moment, wondering exactly how he saw her jaded, worldly-wise, self. Men had controlled her life over the years, though she had learned by now how to sway their decisions. Men controlled the world, yet they were easily influenced by women like her. It had become a habit to assess her effects on men as conversations proceeded.

What had been a defensive mechanism in the first place was now a major source of positive progress towards the things she wanted in life. 'James Turner is violent towards Peg Reynolds. I'm sure that if you saw the whole of her body, you'd find bruises which come from him. When he's frustrated he hits her – probably just because she's the nearest person who matters to him. I've never been great on psychology, particularly where violence is concerned. I expect people who are violent in one context are well capable of being violent in another. But you'd have more experience of that than I have.'

Hook didn't comment on that. He looked at Lambert, who immediately said, 'We now have certain information which you chose to withhold from us when we spoke about Samuel Jackson's murder on Wednesday.'

She turned her attention back to the big cheese, wondering if these two were employing their own sophisticated version of the good-cop bad-cop strategy. 'I didn't give you the story of my life. It would have taken too long and been rather boring. If I withheld something you now think is interesting, it was because it had no connection with Sam's death.'

She managed a smile, but she was suddenly looking strained again because of this unexpected attack from the lined, massively experienced face above her. What was it they knew about her and Sam which she would rather have concealed? Lambert shook his head abruptly, dismissively. 'This is highly relevant to Jackson's death. It is a piece of information he was prepared to use against you, I think. And possibly against someone else in the *Herefordshire Horrors* cast as well.'

'You had better tell me what you're talking about instead of playing games with me. Then I shall tell you why it has no connection with what has happened this week.'

'With two ruthless killings, you mean. This is not a time for euphemisms, Miss Rokeby.'

She chose her words carefully, hoping that they knew less than she feared they did. 'Sam knew about a relationship I'd had with his leading man in the Inspector Loxton series, Martin Buttivant. It was a long time ago, when we were both very young. It had no connection with Sam's death.'

'It was a little more than a relationship that Sam Jackson

was aware of and was using against you. I have to tell you that Mr Clark was in possession of the same information. He appears to have been privy to almost everything which Mr Jackson knew. As producer and assistant producer, they obviously exchanged all information which they thought was relevant and useful to them.'

So what she and Martin thought of as their secret hadn't died with Sam Jackson, as they had both presumed when they spoke on Wednesday. Clark had known all about it, and his death last night hadn't released them. He'd left things behind which these quietly insistent men were now aware of. Sandra said dully, hopelessly, 'You're right. It wasn't just the relationship between Martin and me that Sam and apparently Eric knew about. He could hardly have blackmailed us with that, which was what in effect he was doing.'

'You'd appeared in a porn movie together in 1987.' Let's have that on the table and move forward, Lambert thought impatiently.

'Yes. We were very young and very stupid. I was nineteen or twenty and Martin was just a little older, but still completely unknown and unsuccessful as an actor. I'd had my tits on page three and not much beyond that; I was still trying to get into acting. You took whatever you could get as youngsters trying to scratch a living out of a profession which didn't want you. That's how it felt. We took a porn movie because it was the only thing that had been offered to us in months. The maker of it knew that we were an item at the time so that it was nothing new for us to get our kit off and give each other one with enthusiasm – I remember that phrase even now, you see. The only thing different is that there would be a discreetly placed camera, he said. By today's standards it was pretty mild stuff and it didn't pay much, but we were both desperate for money and even more desperate for any kind of work in the profession. I can see now that it was hardly that, but it seemed like some sort of stepping stone into professional acting at the time.'

'We're not interested in taking high moral ground, Miss Rokeby. We're interested in any connection this might have had with the murders of Samuel Jackson and Ernest Clark.'

It sounded odd to hear Sam and Ernie named formally like that. More threatening, somehow. She said as brightly as she could, 'That's good, then. Because it had nothing to do with either of these deaths.'

'That porn movie was being used against you, wasn't it?'

She smiled, still pale beneath her minimal make-up. 'I've had worse things to contend with than that over the last twenty-five years.'

'Maybe. But Sam Jackson and Ernie Clark knew that publicising the fact that you appeared in something like that would seriously affect your career and even more seriously affect Martin Buttivant's career.'

She looked at him as coolly as she could. 'It's a motive, I suppose. We knew all about it with Sam because he used anything that he could against you. Sometimes it would be to keep your salary down when you had a recurring role, as Martin had. Sometimes it would be to make you appear in a particular episode when you had other plans for the summer, as I had.' She didn't see how they could contest that, whether they believed her or not. 'I didn't know that Ernie Clark knew about it; I don't imagine Martin did, either. So it's not a motive for killing him for either of us, so far as I can see.'

'Unless one or both of you found out that Mr Clark knew about the porn movie between Jackson's death on Tuesday and his shooting last night.'

'I didn't. I don't suppose Martin Buttivant did either. I know I didn't kill Ernie and I should be astounded if Martin had done it.'

'This would have been a convenient joint killing. If you had enticed Mr Clark here, for instance, and Mr Buttivant had put the bullet in his head.'

Sandra flinched instinctively at the image. She said rather desperately, 'And where would we have acquired a pistol, if that's what it was that killed Ernie?'

'I don't know that. Do you or Mr Buttivant own a pistol?'

'I don't. Any sort of firearm has always scared me. I wouldn't have one in my house. I imagine Martin feels much the same. We're actors, Mr Lambert. We deal all the time in make-believe, not in genuine violence.'

'And yet one of you actors seems to have committed two murders in a week. Whom do you suspect, Miss Rokeby?'

'I don't know. That's your job, not mine. I wish you'd get on with it. It's not pleasant, looking round the table at dinner and wondering which of your companions might be a killer.'

THIRTEEN

David Deeney phoned his partner in Oxford. It was a fraught exchange, because Deeney was in the grip of a cold, dangerous annoyance he couldn't remember feeling in years. 'I didn't even know you'd seen me dumping those trainers. You certainly shouldn't have mentioned it to the police. Not without contacting me first.'

Trevor Fisher sounded like a boy who had been doing his best in an alien adult world, not a mature man. 'I didn't know that. You hadn't said anything to me. I was trying to help the young officer who took my statement. She was very young. Her uniform looked brand new. She's just making her way in a new career, I think. I was just trying to give her what help I could.'

David wanted to yell at him for his naivety, to scream at him that he must grow up and live in the real world. The innocence, the unawareness of the darker elements in life had been part of the man's attraction for him when they had got together. It now seemed not only tiresome but dangerous. He forced himself to speak evenly, feeling as though he was conforming to a part in a play rather than expressing his real feelings. 'These are police officers, Trevor, whether they're the grizzled chief super I've been dealing with or the newest recruit who apparently was sent out to see you. Their job is to arrest people. If they see the chance of pinning a crime on someone and making an arrest, they're on to it in a flash. They talk about justice and the long arm of the law, but what they want are arrests and convictions.'

'You're very cynical. We're in Britain, not some third -world country. It is our duty to help the police. I thought that you believed in that.'

David took two very deep breaths before he replied. He was abruptly aware that their whole relationship was at stake here and suddenly conscious that he did not want to lose this wonderfully innocent and unspoiled man from his life. 'You didn't do anything wrong, not really. It's just that we've had two murders in our midst in the last three days and things are very fraught here. We're all looking round and wondering which of us might be mixed up in this. Which of us might even have killed two people.'

'What's your schedule for today?'

'I'm in the first scene we're shooting on location. Then I should be free for most of the rest of the day. Unless the bloody police collar me again, of course. I'm now a leading suspect, thanks to you.' He couldn't resist the barb; he was reminding the man he loved that his wretched innocence could be a liability amidst the blood and iron which characterized the real world.

Trevor said, 'I'll drive over and see you. I'm due a break from my work, anyway. And I've a quiet day today. I was translating stuff for ten hours yesterday, so I've earned myself a break.'

Why did a man in his thirties have to be so damned conscientious, sounding like a dutiful child? Working from home and earning his living as he did from translations, Trevor was his own boss. But David wanted to see Trevor, to assure him that things were all right in the long term, that this wasn't going to be allowed to spoil things. Unless . . . That train of thought was better left unexplored. 'I don't want you coming to the location site. Meet me in Ross-on-Wye. By the old market cross in the centre. Twelve o'clock?'

'Midday would be ideal for me. I'll be there. And I'm sorry.'

Fisher stood looking at his phone for a moment after David had rung off. He'd always known acting was a strange profession, totally alien to him. He was wondering now quite how strange, and whether he should ever have got involved with someone so deeply immersed in it.

On the location site near Oldford, David Deeney was donning his dog collar and mentally easing himself into the role of vicar. He wasn't addressing a congregation in the ancient country church in this scene, but talking with his stage wife and two other women in the vicarage. One of the good things about acting was that you had to forget everything else to do it successfully. Unless you shut out the rest of your life and everything that had happened in the last few days, you wouldn't be able to play the character as the script required you to do. Concentration had now become a mercy as well as a necessity.

The vicar who had been so convincing as a man who could communicate with his flock in the church scene he had filmed on Wednesday had another, less public, dimension to demonstrate in this scene. He needed to be enigmatic, to give the merest suggestion that there might be a more sinister side to him. Fortunately, people were quite prepared to consider that clergymen might be morally suspect nowadays, after the revelations of the last few years. Paedophilia and deceit were everywhere among people of the cloth, according to the followers of the more sensationalist tabloids. Nothing was what it seemed and even the most conventional, pious statements should not be accepted at face value.

David Deeney privately deplored this cynicism in the public, but he found it useful to him this morning as he tried to suggest the many layers of the clergyman he was playing in *Herefordshire Horrors*. He delivered his unremarkable lines to his wife in a thoroughly conventional way, then introduced a subtle change in tone as he talked to the other women. He was talking about parish matters, but the movements of his eyes suggested a hidden and more devious purpose. There might be a sexual suggestion, even lechery, behind his innocent words, or so the impish brown eyes suggested.

David enjoyed making his vicar more enigmatic, enjoyed injecting the subtle shaft of danger into his bearing. This was a murder mystery, after all, and the vicar by the end of the proceedings was to be one of the suspects. But you must be subtle: the merest facial suggestion was enough, for a television audience. This was a modern detective mystery, not a Victorian melodrama being played for laughs. People sitting comfortably in front of their television sets must be puzzled, not amused or outraged.

It took Deeney a couple of minutes to shrug off his television persona after the take was successfully concluded. He folded his dog collar and cassock carefully away in the wardrobe department and offered the girl there a few kind words; it always paid to keep in with the wardrobe staff if you wanted your costumes to fit exactly and becomingly. He sighed as he went out to his car; the real problems of David Deeney were so much more pressing and pertinent than those of the character he was leaving behind. He was almost glad that he had to park a street or two away from his destination. Locking up his car and walking slowly and deliberately up the slope to the meeting place he had suggested gave him a little time to calm his mind and organize what he wanted to say.

Trevor Fisher was waiting for him in the market square at Ross-on-Wye when he arrived there. David said simply, 'I'm glad you came.'

He meant it and it was the right thing to say. Trevor smiled and visibly relaxed. He would never have made an actor, David thought happily. He was far too honest and transparent. There was no malice in him, and without a knowledge of malice, as well as of a lot of other vices, you would always be limited as an actor. Trevor said, 'I'm sorry again about the trainers. I didn't know I wasn't supposed to mention them to the police. You should have told me that.'

He was like a large, well-meaning child. Unless you knew him well, you would never realize what an intelligent, thinking, caring man he also was, thought David. He said, 'It doesn't matter. Not really. It caused me a certain amount of embarrassment with the police. It wasn't something I could easily explain away.'

'Why did you need to explain it away, David?'

He wouldn't understand, of course he wouldn't. Tell the truth and shame the devil was something Trevor Fisher had learned in childhood and observed ever since. And it had served him surprisingly well. He was a respected member of the intelligentsia in Oxford where he worked, respected for his facility in four different languages. Translating at home wasn't especially lucrative, but it was the right occupation for him. He would never have risen in any business in the city, because he would never tell the small lies and do the small, mean actions which might get him ahead of others. But Fisher was happy with what he did, far happier than he would be if he'd had to work with others and accept their foibles and weaknesses. Happy is he who is without pettiness and has found an occupation which will accommodate him, thought David Deeney. He took his lover's hand and said, 'It will be all right, Trevor, really it will. Let's find somewhere where we can get a bite to eat.'

They found a small café which served light lunches and sat in a quiet alcove where they could talk. David had felt exposed, even for an instant ashamed, as he had taken Trevor's hand with people hurrying past them in the market square, but that was something he would never be able to explain to Trevor. Instead, he said, 'It's all been very fraught in the hotel, since Sam Jackson was killed on Tuesday. It's going to be even more so, now that we've lost Ernie Clark.'

'He was murdered too, not just lost, you said.' It was characteristic of Fisher that he could not accept even that small evasion.

'Yes. Everyone is on edge. Everyone is looking at the others across the table and wondering what they know.'

'It must be horrid for you. Have you any idea who killed these men?'

'No.'

'You didn't like them, did you? You didn't like either of them.'

It was a statement, not a question. David wondered what implications his partner was drawing from it. He tried a full, patient explanation. 'No one liked Sam Jackson. We worked with him because we had to do that or not work at all. He had the money to finance things. Finance is a permanent problem in the theatre and in drama generally. Plays are expensive things to produce, particularly if they have big casts and varied locations. That's why so many things in the theatre now have only three or four actors. Television has potentially a much wider audience and thus more potential, but drama is still the most expensive thing it does. That's why more and more of it is bought in from independent companies. That's why people like Sam Jackson are more powerful than they've ever been: there aren't many people around prepared to put up the money for risky projects.'

He couldn't remember if he'd said any of this to Trevor before. Probably not; Fisher had always shied away from theatre talk, as he said it made him feel very ignorant. It was more likely that he felt sullied by such things, thought David Deeney resentfully. Some of us have to live in the real world so that others can refuse to be soiled by it. That wasn't fair; Trevor didn't earn as much as he was bringing in at the moment, but he earned enough, and he brought it home regularly and reliably, unlike all but a very few actors.

Trevor said, 'Sam Jackson didn't like people like us, did he?'

David shrugged, perhaps a little too elaborately. 'Sam didn't like anyone, as far as I could see. He used whatever he could to insult people and keep them in their subordinate places. In my case, it was my homosexuality. If I hadn't been gay, he'd have found something else; he was that sort of man.'

'Homosexuality.' Trevor enunciated the seven syllables carefully and slowly. 'It must be horrible when someone who controls your life treats you like that. It must make you very angry. It must make you want to kill him.'

It was spoken quietly but very deliberately. It was no more than speculation, but it rang like an accusation over the slice of cheesecake which Trevor was dividing carefully with his cake fork. Deeney's brown eyes looked hard into Fisher's blue ones for seconds which seemed to stretch painfully long. 'You're right. It did make me angry. But I've met with lots of that sort of thing over the years and I've learned to grind my teeth and ignore it. I didn't kill Sam Jackson.'

'No, of course you didn't. I never thought you did. But why get rid of a perfectly good pair of trainers which were scarcely worn?'

He was like a child picking at a scab because he could not leave it alone. He really doesn't live in the real world, David thought irritably. 'Because it seemed rational to me at the time to do that. The police obviously considered me a suspect. I would have done the same, in their position. I'd worn those trainers when I'd been to see Sam in his caravan within hours of his death. I watched the scene of crime team picking up soil samples from the carpet in there and from the steps outside and I knew that some of it, perhaps all of it, must have come from the soles of my shoes. I felt threatened. The logical thing at the time seemed to be to ditch the shoes.'

He'd almost said 'the evidence', but that would have been the wrong word to use with Trevor.

Fisher said, 'You didn't like Ernie Clark either, did you?'

Deeney wanted to deny that, but he knew he must have said it to Trevor Fisher at some time, for that very literal man to be quoting it at him now. He wished in a frantic second of self-knowledge that he could be as honest and straightforward as his companion. 'No, I didn't. I'm not quite sure why. He didn't go out of his way to be deliberately offensive, like Sam. I think he just didn't much like actors. It's emerging now that he knew everything that Sam knew about all of us. I suppose we should have expected that. As producer and assistant producer, they had mutual interests; the secrets which gave Sam power over us could be just as useful to Ernie, if he chose to use them.'

'And someone's now killed Ernie.'

Trevor was looking full into his face as he said it. It seemed again like an accusation, but it might have been no more than a genuine curiosity – after all, not many people had to deal with murder once in their lives, let alone twice in three days. David said carefully, 'Yes they have. Last night, it seems, from what I was able to gather from the others. He wasn't staying in the hotel, but he came there in his car. The rumour is that someone shot him.' He'd chosen that word 'rumour' deliberately. It somehow seemed to make the crime more distant from him than if he'd stated it as an established fact. 'The police were swarming all over the hotel and the car park when I left to go for the filming at the location site.'

'Who killed him, David?'

A question was better than a direct accusation, David supposed, but only just. 'I don't know, do I? I'd have been straight in to tell the police if I had, wouldn't I?'

Trevor Fisher didn't respond to that. He couldn't rid himself of that persistent image of David dumping the trainers in their rubbish to be destroyed for ever. He said, 'I've given myself the day off. Do you want to meet again later?'

Deeney said rather woodenly, 'That would be nice. I'll need to get back to the hotel to eat with the others this evening, but we could meet for a cup of tea at around half past four, I should think. There's a place by the river, towards the bottom end of the town.'

John Watts was even more briskly efficient than usual. As director, he was normally in charge of location shooting and everyone accepted that he would be the driving force behind the day's progress. But with the demise of first Jackson and now Clark, he had taken on responsibility for the whole enterprise and become the person whom everyone depended on to make sure that *Herefordshire Horrors* did not founder in these most dangerous of seas.

He gave terse, useful instructions to the man and the three women in the first scene of the day, in which David Deeney's vicar spread his wings and showed unexpected aspects of his character. The scene was short enough for him to review the rushes and pronounce it a successful take before he gave his final instructions to set up the furnishings and props for the second scene of the day, where Sandra Rokeby and Sir Bradley Morton were to confront each other unexpectedly in a stable, of all unlikely places. Then he strode briskly to the hut designated as the murder room, anxious to fulfil his obligations to the CID in what was for him an inevitably busy day.

He glanced at his watch even as he accepted their invitation to sit before them, indicating that he was fulfilling what he saw as a tiresome but necessary duty. 'Please make this as brief as possible. You will no doubt accept that I must be even more busy than usual, in the light of what happened to Ernie Clark last night.'

'You're taking over the producer's responsibility for the series?' Lambert raised his eyebrows elaborately, though he was by no means surprised.

Watts smiled, his thin face a picture of repressed energy. He had trimmed his small beard, so that it no longer waggled extravagantly when he spoke vigorously. 'For this episode certainly. Possibly for future Inspector Loxton series, if things work out that way.'

'You've been quick to seize control. It's almost as if you had been expecting Mr Clark to meet the fate which had already overtaken Samuel Jackson.'

He refused to bridle in the face of this attack. The man was trying to rile him and make him reveal things, but he would not succeed. 'Someone has to take over. Someone has to hold everything together. There weren't many candidates: actors are not the best organizers, as you may have noted by now, chief superintendent.'

His deep-set grey eyes seemed almost taunting. Certainly they were watching closely and missing nothing that was available to them, here as elsewhere on the location site. It was Bert Hook who now said quietly, 'Did you ask Mr Clark to meet you in the hotel car park last night?'

'No. Why would I do that?'

'To kill him and engineer the situation which you are now exploiting.'

'That's outrageous!' John was genuinely annoyed now, forgetting the resolution he had made as he came here to keep calm and dispose of this necessary evil swiftly and without excitement. 'The very idea that I would do such a thing is preposterous!'

'Preposterous or not, someone seems to have done just that. It's our job to find which one of a relatively small number it was. You are the one who seemed most prepared for the event, the one who has taken over Mr Clark's role in addition to your own. You have just told us that actors are not generally fitted for that role. You have virtually invited us to consider you as a leading suspect for murder, Mr Watts.'

It was logical enough when put like that, John supposed. But these thoughts seemed more astounding when they came from the mouth of that stolid, unthreatening presence, which looked as if it should be in uniform and riding a bike round a village in a 1950s' Ealing comedy. 'I didn't kill Sam Jackson and I didn't kill Ernie Clark. I should like that formally recorded.'

Hook smiled over his notebook. 'I can only record that you deny it, Mr Watts. We hope to be able to record the facts of the matter within the next thirty-six hours.'

It was always rather chilling for suspects if you mentioned

exact times, in Bert's experience. It wouldn't do any harm to suggest to this competent, well-organized man that they were contemplating an early arrest. 'Mr Jackson stayed with Mr Clark in his house in Gloucester on the night before he was murdered here. They don't appear to have had any secrets from each other.'

He managed to make that sound quite threatening, even though John Watts hastened to say, 'I wouldn't have expected them to, as producer and assistant producer. The Ben Loxton series is a great success, but they had a lot at stake as a partnership, here and elsewhere.'

'Yes. Mr Clark kept certain notes on his director and the members of his cast. Things which he thought might be useful to him, we must suppose. I expect most of them were passed on to him by Samuel Jackson, who seems to have revelled in such knowledge.'

'Sam loved to revile people and humiliate them. He loved it even more when he could discover things in their lives which they would rather have kept hidden. Knowledge was power, he said. It enabled him to keep salaries down and do what he wanted to actors rather than allow what they wanted. That was why you had a wide range of possibilities for his killer. We were all shocked, because we do not see our acquaintances and friends as killers, but we were not surprised about the victim. Frankly, most of us were not distressed by Jackson's death.'

'Whereas you were by Ernie Clark's?'

John took his time, knowing that he had led himself into this. 'He wasn't as obviously hostile as Sam. He didn't take an open delight in discomforting people. But you tell me he knew everything Sam knew, so I suppose whoever killed Sam would have almost the same reason to kill Ernie.'

'Exactly the same reason, in fact. What do you think happened to Mr Jackson's mobile phone, Mr Watts?'

John felt as though his heart had stopped for a moment, then lurched on. 'I don't know. I didn't see him use it very much.'

'Really? That seems surprising, in someone who was Jackson's chosen director and had been for several years. Mr Clark seems to have been speculating on where his partner's phone might have disappeared to when he met his own death.'

'I can't think where it would have gone. Perhaps the person who killed him took it away.'

'That seems extremely likely to us also, Mr Watts. That's why we should like to know who disposed of it.'

'Sam knew a lot of things about a lot of people. Unsavoury things. I can well imagine that if someone had spoken to him on his phone, whoever it was might have wished to remove all trace of that conversation, especially when Sam became a murder victim and the police were investigating his possessions.'

'Yes. The person with the best opportunity to remove a personal phone from his possession would be the person who discovered his body, wouldn't you think?'

John Watts felt panic now, but he kept his cool nonetheless. 'No. I would think the person who killed him had the best opportunity to take the phone away, and probably the best motive to do that.'

'Correct. The person who killed Jackson might also be the person who affected to discover the body, of course. We have to bear that in mind. What do you know about that phone, Mr Watts?'

He was persistent as well as perceptive, this stolid-looking sergeant. Watts was conscious of Lambert's intense face also, with the clear grey eyes watching him for minutes on end, seeming never to blink. He had the feeling that they knew things about him, knew about that phone and what he had done with it. Were they trying to trap him into a denial? You never knew quite what they had discovered from their relentless questioning of the other people involved and their searching of Ernie Clark's house. He said very quietly, scarcely believing he was voicing this, 'I disposed of that phone. I took it from Sam's pocket when I found him dead on Tuesday. I drove out after dark and flung it from a bridge into the Severn near Tewkesbury.'

'And why did you do that, Mr Watts?' Hook sounded as if he had known of that journey on Tuesday night from the start, though it was in fact the first he had heard of it.

'Sam knew things about me. He knew that I'd told lies, said

that I had directing experience which I did not have. It was when I was a young man and desperate to get work. He'd spoken of it to me the night before he died, reminding me that he knew, reminding me that if I wanted to go on working for him I wasn't to expect a rise in salary. I thought the record of that call would show up on his mobile account and reveal that I had a motive to kill him. When I found his corpse, the phone was actually sticking out of his pocket. It seemed almost an invitation to remove it and dispose of it.'

The three men were silent for a moment, picturing the scene he had described. Each of them knew that it was a short leap from that to the image of the murderer standing over the strangled corpse of Samuel Jackson, wondering what there was left in the caravan which might incriminate him.

Lambert had not spoken for a long time. He now said, 'Do not leave the hotel where you are staying without giving us full information on your intended movements, Mr Watts.'

FOURTEEN

Sir Bradley Morton had agreed to visit the murder room for further talks with CID at four in the afternoon. He should be finished with filming commitments by then, he assured them. Meanwhile, he had more important things to do.

Sandra Rokeby had agreed to drive him into Gloucester. He hadn't brought his own car to the location shooting: there was no problem getting to and from the hotel, as lots of other people in the cast and crew had cars. He only missed his car on occasions like this, when he felt the lack of independence. His wife had always been prepared to run him about, but she'd been gone for years now. He wondered idly as he sat beside Sandra whether she was still happy with her new man, and found himself hoping that she was. Well, that was good; he'd have been much more bitchy about her at one time. Perhaps age really did mellow you, as some of his favourite authors maintained it should do.

Sandra was normally very lively and at ease with Brad, but the conversation was muted on this bright, warm morning. Probably both of them were inhibited by what had happened to Ernie Clark last night. They did not speculate on who might have killed him; both of them had a feeling that such a line of speculation was better avoided. He gave her precise directions as they ran into the ancient city with its towering cathedral.

'You know this neck of the woods well,' Sandra said as she waited at traffic lights.

'It's where I began life.' Then after a pause: 'And where I shall end it, I expect.'

'But not for a good few years yet, I trust!' said Sandra Rokeby conventionally.

'Are you glad to be rid of Ernie Clark?' asked Brad, brutally and suddenly.

She had not expected anything as direct as this, particularly when they had hardly spoken for the first few miles. 'I was glad to see Sam off the scene. I think we all were,' she said. It was an evasion, she knew, an excuse for not answering him directly about last night's death. But old Brad was a lovable rogue, not a detective, wasn't he? Sandra said, 'Ernie was nothing like as nasty and vindictive as Sam. But he knew all the things Sam knew, didn't he, and he was prepared to exploit them in the same way. I wasn't quite prepared for that.'

Sir Bradley smiled grimly. 'We work in a nasty business, don't we?'

Sandra eased the car carefully forward through the crowded central streets of Gloucester. 'No nastier than many others, I suspect. People do whatever is necessary to strengthen their own positions in many walks of life, I fancy.'

He glanced at his watch as they pulled into the hospital car park. 'I shouldn't be long. He normally keeps pretty strictly to his appointment times.'

'One of the advantages of going private, I expect.' She hadn't asked him why they had come here and he hadn't told her. Unusual, that. Old Brad didn't have many inhibitions or keep many secrets from her. They'd been friends since he'd made his first pass at her and she'd laughingly rejected it. That was more years ago than she cared to recall this morning.

He said, 'You need BUPA or something similar, in our trade. You can't afford to be unavailable if there's work around.'

'Unless you're a knight of the realm and a national institution, with people clamouring to employ you.' A little flattery never went amiss, even between old friends.

'I'm going now, before I find you irresistible and leap upon you,' he said with dignity. 'There's a coffee bar near the entrance.'

'I shall probably just get myself a paper and wait here for you.' She felt suddenly serious and solemn. After all, she had no idea what he was here for.

He took care to throw his shoulders back and walk very upright as he strode into the place. Always present yourself at your best: the actor's adage. A woman recognized him in the reception area, but he was past her and into the lift before she could speak to him, staring straight ahead in the manner cultivated by all show business people.

The man he had come to see hadn't followed that tenet about presenting himself carefully. His hair could have done with a comb and he needed a shave. But Brad knew he was an eminent man in his field, which was all that mattered. The consultant stood behind his desk and offered his hand. 'We could take a blood test,' he said, with the air of a man who knows that his options are limited.

'There's no point,' said Sir Bradley Morton. 'We both know the score. I just need more pills.'

'It's your choice,' the specialist said uneasily. He understood the actor's thinking exactly, but his instinct, his training and his whole professional ethos were to preserve human life for as long as possible. 'It's my duty to encourage you still to consider chemotherapy. I might—'

'Bollocks, Mr Dunne!' said Brad crisply. 'It's not your duty to repeat yourself and it's not my duty to listen. Will the pain get worse?'

'It needn't do, not appreciably. If you up the dose as the pain increases, it will shorten life but make it bearable. Morphine's a killer, ultimately. But it kills pain too.'

'I'll up the dose, don't you worry about that. I'm a fully paid-up coward, when it comes to pain. As far as I can tell, it's not affecting my work so far.'

'There's no reason why it should do, at this point.' In truth, Dunne didn't know how well an actor could cope at this stage of the illness; that aspect was a new experience for him as well as his patient. 'I expect "Doctor Theatre" helps you to cope.'

Bradley Morton smiled. 'That's easier when you're literally in a theatre and there's an audience to interact with. We're filming on location for the *Inspector Loxton* television series at present, so you've only a camera and a director to keep happy. But I'm such an old ham that it hasn't been a problem for me. Bit of a shame that the nation will never see my shot at *King Lear*, but I've been pretty lucky in my acting life, really.'

That was a final piece of vanity; Brad knew in his heart of hearts that he would never have been asked to play Lear. This time it was he who stood and offered his hand to the professional behind the desk. They gripped and held for a fraction longer than they had done when he arrived, for each of them knew that it would be the last time.

Dunne remained still in his chair for a moment after the ageing actor had left. People often seemed to acquire a new dignity when death was inevitable.

Whilst Sir Bradley Morton was contemplating the end of his life as an actor, a woman who had only recently embarked upon that journey was having a difficult time with John Lambert and Bert Hook. Peg Reynolds felt inexperienced and very susceptible in the face of this very considerable detective experience.

'You took dinner in the hotel about an hour after most of the rest of the cast.' Lambert issued the simple statement as if it were a challenge

'Someone told you that, did they? I expect they enjoyed doing it.' Peg was trying to be aggressive, but aggression did not sit happily upon her.

'We ask questions and people answer them. It's the way the system works. If people behave as if they have something to hide, it excites our interest. Why did you choose not to eat with your colleagues and to eat later than them?'

For a moment, she toyed with the idea of telling them she had been rolling naked on the bed with James and offering them every detail of their violent congress. It would be thrilling to shock these two older men. But they didn't look as if anything could shock them. Keep to the truth as far as possible, people said, when you have things to conceal. Unnecessary lies are just an additional source of danger. 'We argued, my boyfriend and I. We seem to spend a lot of time arguing nowadays. Far too much, I'm sure.'

The phrases carried a ring of finality, of an acceptance that there must be closure, but Lambert ignored that for the moment. He glanced down at a note from DI Rushton. 'Your boyfriend is James Turner.'

'Yes. Your lot have interviewed him. You've asked him all sorts of questions, though it was obvious that he couldn't have killed Sam Jackson.'

'He had to be eliminated, as had thirty or so other people. It's the way we proceed.'

'And now you have a second murder. Your procedures don't seem very effective.' It was a cheap jibe, but one she couldn't resist. She was still very young and in this situation she felt even younger.

'And now we have to eliminate you from suspicion of the killing of Ernest Clark – assuming that is possible.'

'I didn't kill Sam and I didn't kill Ernie. What reason would I have to wish either of them dead?'

'Ambition, perhaps.'

'I'm doing all right in a crowded profession, thank you very much. Sam wasn't going to stop me and neither was Ernie. I'm getting good reviews and plenty of offers. I'm sorry if that sounds like boasting, but I'm telling you that I didn't need the approval of Messrs Jackson and Clark.'

Others in the cast had said she was good. And she had the looks which always helped talent along. Dark, lustrous hair which concealed just enough of her neck to make it more desirable, and huge brown eyes which seemed to comprehend so much more than they actually saw. But she was nervous, very nervous: much more so than she had been when they spoke with her on Wednesday.

Lambert said quietly, 'Ambition can embrace others as well as ourselves, Miss Reynolds. I believe you were trying to secure acting work for Mr Turner.'

Who had been talking, Peg wondered. She thought she had been discreet, but actors always seemed to know. Perhaps it was the fact that almost all of them had been through the mill themselves, wondering at times where the next job was coming from, which made them sensitive to the efforts of others to find work. 'I made enquiries on behalf of James, yes. It's natural when you love someone that you would do that.'

'And you love James Turner?'

'Who knows what love is, chief superintendent? Even

someone with your experience might not care to offer us a definition.'

She forced a smile to gild that thought. It was a brave effort, in the circumstances. Bert Hook shifted a little so as to look directly into her face. 'Would you care to show us your upper arms, Miss Reynolds?'

'No, I would not! Is this the kind of request you are in the habit of making when you interview a younger woman?'

'No, it is both irregular and unusual. But I have a particular reason for asking the question. We believe that James Turner has offered physical violence to you.'

He was almost fatherly, she thought, speaking as if he could barely control his regret. She said aggressively, 'Who told you this?'

'That is confidential. Just as whatever you tell us in the next few minutes will remain confidential from others we shall speak with.'

'James has been under a lot of strain. And what happens between us should remain between us.'

'Possibly. Though if violence is involved, that may not be so. But we're investigating two murders, and we need to know whether your relationship with your boyfriend has a connection with either of them.'

'It doesn't. I asked Sam about work for James, pleaded for him to have even a small part in the Ben Loxton series. Jackson laughed in my face. Then he leered at me and asked if I was proposing to prostitute my talents in pursuit of employment for an oaf without ability. We both knew what he meant, though I can't think he expected to be taken seriously.'

'You must have been glad when he died and happy to have a new man in charge. Did you approach Ernie Clark to try to get work for Turner?'

'No. I was planning to, but I didn't get the chance, did I?'

'Didn't you? Someone almost certainly arranged to meet Mr Clark in the car park at your hotel last night. You were separated from your acting colleagues, both in the early part of the evening and after you had eaten dinner. Did you meet Mr Clark then?'

'No. I had no reason to do so.'

'You've just given us a reason why you wished to see him. You wished to speak with him alone, to plead the case of James Turner for work in this or one of his other projects.'

'I'd have put the case for James, yes, given the chance. I didn't arrange to meet Ernie last night and I don't know who killed him.'

'You'd better give us an account of your movements during the evening.'

'James and I were in my room until we went down for dinner. That was some time later than the others, as you said.'

'Does Mr Turner have a room of his own?'

'No. But mine is a double. Whoever booked the rooms for us was generous: they are the best ones in the hotel, I think. But then the Inspector Loxton series is highly successful, so that they can afford to keep people happy. I expect it's good policy to do that.'

'You said you argued in the hour before you went for dinner. Was that in your room?'

'Yes. Where else would it be?'

Hook ignored that. 'So there is no one who can confirm that you were alone with Mr Turner in your room at that time?'

'Only James himself. And I suppose you won't accept that. You'd rather postulate some sinister conspiracy between us to dispose of Ernie Clark.'

In fact, in the absence of other evidence, they'd have to accept what she said. It was the equivalent of a husband-wife alibi; the word of spouses was always suspect, but there was nothing the police could do about that unless they could unearth contradictory information from some other source. 'What did you do after the meal, Peg?'

It was the first use of her Christian name by either of them. It dropped oddly, almost harshly, into this context, but Hook was still looking concerned for her, almost fatherly. They did this kind of thing to get you off your guard, she supposed. She felt absurdly vulnerable. Until this week, she had never in her life been questioned by the police. 'I suggested we joined the others. James didn't want to and I understood that. They'd made him quite welcome at the beginning of the week, but he hadn't responded to that; he has his own problems, you see.'

'You mean that he's hit you and bullied you and that the others know about it and resent it on your behalf. You have friends among the cast of *Hertfordshire Horrors*, Peg. Perhaps it's time you listened to them.'

She refused to meet his eye. 'When we finished dinner, James and I went for a walk beside the river. It was a beautiful tranquil evening and I think we walked a little further than we had intended.'

'Did you notice Mr Clark's car at the end of the car park as you passed it?'

'No. I'm not very interested in cars. James knows a lot more about them than I do. I seem to remember him speaking rather enviously about Ernie's Jaguar, but that might have been earlier in the week.'

'Did you notice any other members of the cast or the crew out there?'

'No. There were certainly other people about, because I remember hearing voices. But whether they belonged to people I knew or to strangers, I couldn't be sure. It was getting quite dark by then and I was preoccupied with my own conversation with James.'

'And what was that about?'

'I can't remember. It certainly wasn't about Ernie Clark.'

Of course she could remember, thought Bert Hook. But she didn't want to tell them, and if it wasn't connected with Clark, it wasn't really their concern. 'Who do you think might have killed Mr Clark?'

'I don't know. If I had any idea, I'd certainly pass it on to you. It's weird looking around at the people you work with and wondering if one of them is a killer in real life. Weird and very unpleasant.'

Hook glanced at Lambert, then accompanied her to the door and beyond it. With blue skies and white clouds above, the world out here was brighter and less threatening. Bert said quietly, 'Get rid of him, Peg, if he hits you. They don't grow out of it. They get worse. We see the results.'

* * *

Back at the hotel by the Wye, the man he was talking about was bored and moody. James Turner had little to occupy him whilst Peg Reynolds was away at the location shooting.

He tried his book, but he found himself reading the same paragraph for a fourth time. He tried writing: he'd written poetry when he was at school and been commended for it by teachers anxious to encourage creativity. But he hadn't kept up the habit, and now when he tried verse for the first time in five years, the words wouldn't come, or were obviously second-hand when they did. He wrote a message to his mother on the postcard he had bought for her, but even that seemed trite and worthless. But postcard messages were supposed to be trite, weren't they? He'd been made to write letters home when he was at his boarding school and he'd become quite good at it over the years. But since the advent of e-mails, letters had almost died out, for him as for millions of others.

He started violently when the phone rang in the quiet room; he must be even more on edge than he'd realized. He composed himself before he picked it up; after all it might be the offer of work for him at last.

It was not. An impassive male voice asked if Peggy Reynolds was available. The phone messages were always for Peg; he should have known it would be for her. He said, 'She's not here at the moment. She's on location filming for the latest episode of the Inspector Loxton series.'

Always let them know that you were working, if you were. It was one of the maxims of the profession. People hiring and firing drew confidence from the knowledge that someone else had thought you were worth employing, had chosen you rather than other candidates. He said on an impulse. 'My name is James Turner. I am Miss Reynolds' partner and agent. Can I be of help?'

'I'm not sure. I really wished to speak to Ms Reynolds directly. You say you are her agent?'

James crossed his fingers metaphorically and plunged on. 'Indeed I am. Peg will not commit herself to anything without discussing it very fully with me beforehand. You will appreciate that her considerable success so far means that she is perpetually having to make decisions about her future. If you can give me as many details as possible of what you are offering, I will make sure that she gives it her full consideration in due course.' The words seemed to come naturally to him. He had started to play this as a game, but he seemed to be rather good at it.

It was a man called Datchet from the Coventry Playhouse and he had an enquiry about Shaw's *Saint Joan*. He became cagey at this point, maintaining that this was all very tentative and that he really needed to speak to Ms Reynolds directly. But Turner knew too much for him. He knew the play and knew that there was only one major female role in it. It was a plum which was being dangled, even for someone as successful as Peg. He said loftily, 'There's only the title role which would be of interest, of course. But I presume that is what you are offering.'

Datchet panicked. He hadn't been empowered to offer the role, only to check that Peg Reynolds was available, along with two or three other possibilities. 'Nothing is definite as yet. Any offer will depend on the availability of the appropriate male actors to appear in the production.'

James tried a cynical laugh and brought it off. 'All of us know that this play is almost unique in demanding the correct casting of the title role. Once you get the right Saint Joan in place, eminent male actors will be queuing up to offer their services.'

'Well, if you could just check for me that Ms Reynolds is available, I'll talk to the theatre management here about exact dates and—'

'Oh, I couldn't even put such a vague proposition forward for Miss Reynolds' consideration.' Turner was gathering confidence as the voice on the other end of the line lost it. 'I suggest that you speak to your masters and come back to us with a firm proposition, Mr Datchet. Dates, length of run, proposed supporting cast and salary. The fuller the detail, the more likely it is that I shall be able to advise Peg Reynolds to consider your offer.'

'I'll do that. I'll get all the detail I can. I'm sorry, but I forgot your name.'

'Turner is my name. James Turner. You may direct any correspondence to me, at Miss Reynolds' address.'

'I'm not sure how far the budget will stretch on this one. It will depend on our total outlay for the year, I presume, and what other productions might cost.'

'Of course it will, Mr Datchet. And art comes before profit with Miss Reynolds; that is why I have to be careful to protect her interests. She has offers on the table from Hollywood agents, offers you could not possibly match. But you should not lose hope: if a theatrical proposition excites Peggy and makes her feel that it would help her to develop and extend her craft as an actor, she will put that before mere money; she has never been a worshipper of Mammon. But Saint Joan is a demanding role, and the rewards will need to be realistic before I can even encourage my client to consider your offer. We shall need everything in writing before we can weigh the pros and cons against other roles which are being offered. I look forward to speaking with you again in the near future, Mr Datchet. In the meantime, thank you for your interest.'

James put the hotel phone down and smiled at it for a long time. He'd positively enjoyed that – the first thing he could remember enjoying in many weeks, apart from the fleeting ecstasy of orgasm. Perhaps he should consider becoming an agent. He had something worthwhile to sell, with Peg. And she needed this kind of protection: if she'd answered the phone, she would have been so pleased to be offered such a plum role at such a reputable theatre that she'd probably have accepted there and then, without even asking about money.

The right questions and the right attitude for an agent had dropped upon him without his needing to think about them. Perhaps that is what he should become: an agent for others, not a perpetually out-of-work actor. He hadn't heard of many agents going bankrupt. Football agents made ridiculous sums. He might not get into that league, but he could make a fat living in show business, if it was all as easy as this. And all this bluff and counter-bluff was really a sort of acting, wasn't it? He wasn't actually deserting his principles.

He went out into the warm day, savouring the light breeze wafting in over the Wye, reliving again the exhilaration of his phone conversation. The lane which had accommodated several couples last night was deserted now. He looked across to the crime scene as he drew level with the end of the car park. The police still had it fenced off, but it looked as if they were preparing to drive Clark's Jaguar away – for further forensic examination, no doubt.

A young uniformed constable was standing beside the driver's door, exactly where James had stood for a moment in the darkness last night.

FIFTEEN

It was early afternoon and Martin Buttivant was feeling quite pleased. He'd successfully completed quite a long scene in the morning and there was only one short exchange with a new young stage constable this afternoon to conclude his work on the location shooting. Most of his serious work was done in the studio. Back there were unchanging models of Inspector Loxton's CID section and home, where his humorous exchanges with his wife showed the lighter, off-duty side of Ben Loxton.

The major task in the day for him was this second interview with the genuine CID bigwigs. It felt very odd for Martin to be involved in a real murder investigation rather than the often sensational fictional ones he investigated as Inspector Ben Loxton. It was even odder to be now a suspect rather than the man in charge of swiftly concluded enquiries. He'd need to be careful, he kept reminding himself. But once he'd negotiated this latest exchange with the fuzz, he'd be able to relax.

Martin installed himself in the chair provided and said, 'You have your job to do and I appreciate that, more than most perhaps. But it would be a help if we could get this over swiftly to allow me to concentrate on my work here.'

'Where you are playing a fictional detective. That must feel rather strange for you, in these circumstances.'

Lambert had echoed his own thought as he stepped into the murder room. 'Yes. I keep feeling I should apologize to you. You're the real thing and I'm a fictional sham, earning more than either of you for pretending to be a detective.'

Lambert smiled grimly. 'The crimes we're investigating are real enough and quite shocking. The context is the only unusual thing for us. I'm approaching the end of a lengthy CID career and it's the first time I've had to investigate a murder among professional actors. And now we have not one killing but two. We also have a diminished number of suspects.

We are satisfied that it was someone staying in the hotel who engineered last night's killing of Ernest Clark, and only the major members of the cast were accommodated there.'

Martin forced a smile. 'It's taken me years to attain that sort of standing. I didn't have it until I secured the role of Ben Loxton, in fact. I've stayed in some pretty grotty places when I've been on location shooting, in the past. Now I've reached the elite and elevated myself to the role of murder suspect at the same time.'

'We'd like to eliminate you from that role, if we can.'

Martin smiled again, trying to show how much at ease he was. He actually felt genuinely relaxed, but he knew that might be dangerous; he needed to stay alert here. 'You sound almost like me as Ben Loxton.' He dropped into a deeper and more sombre voice for his parody. '"We proceed by elimination, sir. If you can provide us with an alibi, we shall be only too pleased to move on to the investigation of others."'

Lambert grinned as he was meant to at the parody, but his steady grey eyes remained fixed on Buttivant's face. 'You didn't like Sam Jackson. You certainly weren't alone in that. How did you get on with Ernie Clark?'

'I didn't know Ernie anything like as well as Sam. He was a more self-effacing character. Sam was in your face the whole time, looking for ways to demean you. There was a method in it – if he could denigrate you and degrade your stature in the profession, he could pay you less. He called it keeping you in your place.'

'Mr Clark was also a producer and therefore presumably also preoccupied with costs and resources. He had the same information which helped to make Samuel Jackson so objectionable and so efficient, didn't he?'

Martin Buttivant told himself to remain alert. They knew more than he had thought they would; perhaps, indeed, they now knew more than he did about the late assistant producer of the Loxton series. 'Yes. It seems to me from what others in the cast have said that Sam Jackson passed on all the squalid information he had gathered over the years to his assistant. I suppose you'd have expected that, but somehow I'd thought that Sam was a one-off, gathering scandal and hugging it to himself rather than keeping his deputy informed of what he was about.'

'Clark knew the same damning facts about you which Jackson had used, didn't he? You hadn't expected that.'

Martin licked his lips. This was a shock. He wasn't a vain man, but playing the leading role in a successful television series made sure that everyone treated you with more respect and consideration than they had previously. People took care not to offend you and that gave you a kind of insulation against criticism. This grave, insistent man had no such inhibitions. 'Ernie knew a lot of things, yes. I think because he'd been self-effacing whilst Sam was around, most of us hadn't expected that. I suppose that was silly; you'd expect a producer to know everything that might work in his favour. But most actors aren't good businessmen. They wouldn't have chosen this profession if they were.'

This was a little ironic, because he'd reminded them a couple of minutes ago that he earned more than either of them. But his point was valid; there were more out-of-work actors than out-of-work policemen. 'You must have been disconcerted to discover how much he knew about you.'

'More than I'd expected him to know, certainly.' His mind was working furiously now, wondering how much he might safely conceal.

'He knew about the porn film you made early in your career with Sandra Rokeby, for instance.'

He told himself that he had known this was coming, but he was shaken nonetheless. He would have denied the episode elsewhere, but there was no point in doing that with the CID. 'Ernie Clark knew about that, yes. Sam had passed the information on to him, or he'd looked through Sam's files. Perhaps I should have expected it, but I didn't.'

'So you arranged to meet him, to discuss how he proposed to use this information – perhaps to do whatever you could to get him to suppress it. You told him you would meet him for a private exchange in the hotel car park last night.'

'No. I might have wanted to meet him in due course, but I arranged nothing last night.'

Lambert nodded slowly. 'You see our problem, Mr Buttivant.

It's pretty clear that someone arranged to meet Mr Clark last night. Then, whether it was premeditated or on impulse, that person killed Mr Clark. Everyone we have spoken to so far denies arranging such a meeting. You are the latest one to do so. Yet you had probably the strongest motive of all for wishing to see Mr Clark permanently silenced.'

'No! I am established in the role of Ben Loxton in what has proved to be a highly successful series. The worst Ernie could have done is to reduce or freeze my salary in exchange for his silence about this youthful escapade.'

There was a pause while the three people in the room weighed the accuracy of the phrase as a summary of Martin Buttivant's appearance with a glamorous member of the *Hertfordshire Horrors*' cast in a squalid sexual romp. Then Hook said quietly, 'There is a rumour that he was contemplating replacing you with a younger actor.'

'That's rubbish! That was never a serious proposition.' Martin was shaken by this quiet, deadly contribution from such an unthreatening source. There is nothing that disturbs an actor more than his replacement in a role in which he considers he has been successful. It shakes him to his roots, apart from any financial implications. It seemed to Buttivant almost obscene that these people from outside the profession should even be aware of the suggestion. Yet they were and this was a murder investigation in which he was centrally involved. This was real life with a vengeance, as opposed to Inspector Loxton. He tried to organize his thoughts. 'Sam issued a vague threat on those lines. I don't believe it was anything more than another of his ploys to hold my salary steady rather than increase it as the series became even more successful. I can't see that such internal squabbles would be of any interest to you.'

Hook raised both eyebrows impressively; it wasn't a move he was inclined to make very often. 'Surely you can see that it is something we have to follow up, when we are investigating murder? It gives you the most obvious of motives. Did Mr Clark propose to implement this threat of replacement?'

How much did they know? Were they tempting him to deny things so that he would place himself in an even more difficult position? Martin made a swift decision that he had much better be honest about this. 'Ernie Clark came here on Wednesday afternoon to check how location filming was going. He said he wished to reassure us that Sam Jackson's death wouldn't make any difference to our present commitments. As we were breaking up for the day and preparing to go back to our hotel, he took me on one side. He made it clear that he knew everything about me that Sam had known. He said that he anticipated that I would continue to work on the series on the same terms as I had already agreed with Sam.'

'Did you accept this?'

'Not in so many words I didn't. It wasn't like signing my name on a contract. But Ernie's expression was "we now both know the score". He was right. I didn't like it, but I had to accept that I stood exactly where I'd stood when Sam was controlling my life.'

'But you didn't like that?'

Martin Buttivant forced a smile he did not feel. 'I expect it sounds like greed to you, wanting more money when I'm already quite well paid. But you must try to understand the strange business in which we actors work. Word gets around. Agents pass information to other agents. Anyone who wishes to know will be able to find out what I earn without much difficulty. There has already been some speculation as to why I am earning in this series exactly what I earned in the last one. When it emerges that I shall be earning no more in next year's series, the rumours will fly and multiply. That won't do my future prospects any good.'

'So you took steps to put things right. You arranged for Ernie Clark to meet you in the hotel car park.'

'No I didn't! I admit that I was very depressed to find that life hadn't changed for me with Sam Jackson's death. But I'd have thought twice about confronting Ernie. Don't forget I've known him for several years now – never as a friend but as an employer. He had a lot less bluster than Sam, but he was in my opinion likely to be much more dangerous as an enemy.'

'In what way dangerous?'

Martin knew he was in too far to withdraw now. He couldn't work out whether being frank was going to make him seem less guilty or more so. 'He had his own gun. I've no idea how long he'd had it, but it was certainly years.'

'What kind of gun?'

'A pistol. We shouldn't call them guns, should we? I've learned that much at least from playing Ben Loxton. A firearm. Definitely a pistol, but I've no idea what sort. We have them on set occasionally – never loaded, of course. But I take no notice of the details of the weapon. I'm strictly an actor, with as little use for a pistol as a Turkish scimitar in real life.'

'So you would have expected Ernie Clark to defend himself last night.'

'If he felt under threat, yes. I can only assume that he felt that there was no danger until it was too late. Perhaps he didn't have his pistol with him, of course. It's a couple of years since he told me he had it and I've no idea if he carried it about with him habitually. For all I know, he kept it locked in a drawer at home and never even thought about it. I'm sure he didn't think of actors as being a physical threat to him.'

'Not even after his immediate superior Sam Jackson had been murdered on Tuesday?'

'Touché, detective sergeant. In the light of that, I'd perhaps have taken my pistol to any meeting if I'd been Ernie Clark, if only as a precaution.'

Lambert, who hadn't spoken for some time, now said very quietly, 'You deny any personal connection with last night's death, Mr Buttivant. So who do you suggest disposed of Ernest Clark so ruthlessly and efficiently?'

'I don't know. I've thought about it, naturally. I'm sure all of us have thought of little else, except when we had work to occupy us. But I am also sure that this death still seems as incredible to my colleagues as it does to me.'

'Yet it's now increasingly probable that one of you was responsible for both of these murders.'

'I have to accept that. It still feels preposterous to me. Perhaps it was one of our support crew who had a grudge against our producers. I'm sure the truth, if it ever comes to light, will be sensational.'

In that at least the man who played Inspector Ben Loxton was correct.

Even on this warm May day, the man wore the brown trilby, which was his trademark. Rather an affectation, that, thought John Watts, as he led the way into his caravan and the privacy they needed for this discussion.

Still, each to his own, and if you dealt for most of your days with actors you were used to affectations. This slightly portly man, who now removed the trilby to reveal thinning, slicked-back hair, watery grey eyes and a small but rather bulbous nose, was not a prepossessing figure. He looked like an unsuccessful shopkeeper. No one would have guessed from his appearance that this was one of the most powerful figures in British drama. The news of Richard Aitchison's judgements travelled quickly around the land and his decisions were rarely overturned.

Money brought power, reflected John Watts. It brought even more power in an industry which was chronically short of capital. Richard Aitchison, relaxing into a situation he felt he knew and understood, seemed suddenly more formidable than he had when levering himself out of his car and blinking in the bright sunlight of the location shooting site, where all was busy activity and everyone but he seemed to know whither they were bound. Aitchison leant back in his chair and smiled a little sourly. Then he looked approvingly at the gin and tonic which had been set on the small table beside him. He did not touch it as yet.

'Bit of a crisis for you, this,' he said with evident satisfaction.

Watts hesitated. You couldn't say that two brutal murders in three days were not a crisis without seeming unfeeling or unrealistic. Aitchison wouldn't greatly mind unfeeling, but he'd frown severely upon the unrealistic. 'From my point of view, it's an inconvenience. No one liked Sam Jackson and I was never close to Ernie Clark. So I'm not stricken by grief. But of course I am shaken by these events, as we all are.'

'Your sentiments do you credit,' said Richard Aitchison dryly. He picked up his glass and savoured his first sip of the gin and tonic.

'I have to be objective rather than sentimental. In these unique circumstances, it seems to me that it is the director's remit to keep the show on the road.'

'An expensive road, when these deaths come in the midst of the large outlays involved in location shooting.'

'Sam Jackson controlled our expenditure pretty tightly, as you can imagine.'

'And Ernie Clark too, I imagine. He had a commendable sense of economy, Ernie.'

'Yes. And I'm happy to say that the police have allowed us to continue shooting here, despite the sensational crimes which have beset us.'

'And despite the fact that you apparently have a murderer within your ranks.' Aitchison sipped again and studied the slice of lemon floating within his cut-glass tumbler, as if the sight of it gave him exquisite satisfaction among these dire happenings.

'Things have gone surprisingly well, in the circumstances. We've had more good first takes than I can remember on any previous location shoot. It's almost as if the exceptional circumstances are making people concentrate on the matter in hand. Perhaps they're relieved to be doing what they know best and what they're here for.'

Aitchison set down his drink and said, 'But you have a financial crisis to contend with. Otherwise I wouldn't be here.'

'I wouldn't call it a crisis. We have a series which is selling all round the world. I have no doubt at all that the *Herefordshire Horrors* will turn out to be another very successful episode amongst that series.'

'It has certainly got a good start in advance publicity, with two murders in your midst and plastered all over the popular press. Public interest when this episode is eventually transmitted should be at an all-time high.'

'It's an ill wind, I suppose.'

'But you need finance.' Aitchison reiterated the thought as if it gave him great satisfaction among minor setbacks like murder.

'We do. But I'm happy to report that it is rather a matter of choosing between competing agencies of support, rather than of trailing round cap in hand searching for angels.'

'How gratifying for you! Perhaps my visit here today is superfluous, though I am thoroughly enjoying your agreeably strong mix of gin and tonic.'

'Never superfluous, Richard! Rather is it that when you have an excellent product to sell you look to the best. And, sparing your blushes, I shall speak quite frankly and tell you that I regard you as the best. You have an unrivalled overview of our business and a proven record of success which now extends over many years.'

Those phrases sounded as if they had been prepared and polished in advance, thought Aitchison. But he had no objection to that. A little deference and a well-honed respect were no bad preliminaries to an investment. 'I might be prepared to offer my financial support, if the terms were suitable. You have as you say a proven product here.' He looked around him and tried to feel at ease. He couldn't remember ever negotiating in a caravan before. But needs must. He was anxious to get in on the Inspector Loxton series, though of course he wouldn't dream of anything so naïve as a revelation of that.

John Watts wasn't going to underplay his own part in sustaining a successful series. He stood to make a lot of money from the week's events and he had thought carefully about how he would go about it. 'I know this series and the cast and technicians involved in it better than anyone else on earth. I shall keep it going during the next few weeks, whatever unwelcome revelations the CID might make to us.'

'That will only have a positive effect, as we have already agreed. The greater the name which is eventually attached to these two killings, the greater and more enduring will be the publicity for not only this episode but for subsequent series.'

That was enough of the preliminary fencing, thought Watts. They both knew why they were here. He knew that Aitchison was a hardheaded businessman, with much more experience of the financing of television drama than he had, but he was determined to turn this situation to his advantage. 'I want in, Richard. I shall continue to direct and I know my cast better than anyone else. I'll exploit this situation, not succumb to it.'

'You're saying that as director of the series you expect a

rise. That would be not unreasonable, in view both of its continuing success and the way in which you seem confident you can handle the present crisis.'

'I want more than that. I want a share in the profits. As a result of what has happened, I have been forced to become more than just a television director, even though my talents in that role will be stretched to their limits by the situation which now confronts me. If and when the mystery of these murders is resolved, I want more control.'

It was what Aitchison had expected. The man most responsible for the success of any television drama series was the director, whatever romantic notions the public held about actors. Actors were important, once they established themselves in roles, because the public grew used to them and resented change. But very few actors were indispensable. It was the director who shaped a series and gave it its distinctive character, who looked ahead beyond particular scenes and even particular episodes and saw how a series might be shaped and developed. Richard had been prepared before he came here for the bid for control and riches that Watts was now making, and had prepared himself for it. 'You're currently earning £300,000 for each series of the Ben Loxton mysteries?'

'Yes. It's been that for the last two series. Sam Jackson didn't believe in spending a penny more than he needed to.'

Aitchison wondered for a moment if Jackson had exercised some control over his director, as he had over most of his actors. But that was not his concern this afternoon. 'It's a generous fee. But not over-generous, in view of the fact that you are now into the fourth series of what has been a highly successful enterprise. Let's assume for the moment that the next series is already funded, whether wholly by me or by a combination of backers. Exactly what are you proposing for yourself?'

'I think it would be not unreasonable for my director's fee to rise to £400,000. But I should be prepared to forgo any rise and put that extra £100,000 into the finances of the enterprise – in effect I would become an angel as well as the director. In exchange, I would expect a fair share of the gross profits from the enterprise.'

'What kind of share?'

This was where John Watts knew he was on tricky ground. With no previous experience of the risks and rewards of financing television drama, he had no real idea what would be a reasonable demand and what would be an outrageous one. 'A quarter of the profits.'

Richard Aitchison smiled patronisingly at such audacity. 'Far too much, John. A tenth might be rather more realistic.'

'I couldn't settle for a tenth – not with the extra risk involved; I'd rather just increase my director's salary.'

Aitchison knew what he was prepared to concede, but of course if he could get away with less he was prepared to do so. They threw figures back and forth for a few minutes and eventually agreed that Aitchison would take over Sam Jackson's role as financer-producer and that Watts would continue on his present director's salary but collect a sixth of future profits.

Aitchison had a second drink and Watts a first one to celebrate the agreement. Both were genuinely happy with the new arrangement. The fewer people who were in control, the better, Richard assured his new acolyte. He thought of Watts as acolyte in terms of financial control, though he generously called him partner as he left the caravan.

The sun was still dazzlingly bright outside, but Richard felt rather less of a stranger and rather more proprietorial as he drove away from the location shoot. A good day's work for both of them, this. He had secured himself the nearest thing to a cast-iron certain profit in a highly uncertain business, and Watts had edged his way into a share of the profits as well as direction.

As he drove away, Richard Aitchison reflected that John Watts was the man who had gained most of all by the two deaths which had occurred this week. It was only at that moment that he found himself hoping fervently that Watts had no connection with them.

SIXTEEN

Four o'clock and the end of what had become for him a very long day. Sir Bradley Morton looked for signs of fatigue in the two CID men and saw none. Perhaps the hospital visit that morning had been more of a strain than it had seemed at the time. He didn't feel that: he'd grown used to the idea of death now. It brought with it a sort of serenity, he felt. But perhaps that was just him being theatrical, as he was about most things. Well, it was sixty years since he'd first trodden the stage as a nervous boy, so a little theatricality was built in and even welcome by now.

Brad said, 'This is a turn-up for the books, isn't it? I wasn't terribly surprised when someone saw fit to dispose of Sam Jackson: he'd been asking for it for years. But Ernie Clark is much more of a surprise.'

Lambert looked at him with undisguised curiosity. 'You do not seem to be unduly shocked by this death yourself, Sir Bradley.'

'Oh, but I am. I suppose that it's just that after a lifetime in this curious business, one disciplines oneself to be shocked by nothing. I remember Larry Olivier saying something on those lines back in the Sixties.'

'Nor do you seem to be devastated by grief.'

'Do you know, that's true! And yet I didn't dislike Ernie. I suppose I was fond of him, with that rather muted affection we accord to non-actors. There is always a sort of invisible barrier between us and those on the fringe of the profession, Chief Superintendent Lambert. We know that someone has to put up the money to allow us to operate, but we rather resent the fact that they take most of the profits without ever exposing themselves to audiences and critics.'

'Men like Jackson and Clark are risk-takers, are they not?'

'Indeed they are. Angels back their judgements and make the profits. But we actors often conveniently forget that they can lose money as well as make it. They have to back the right horse, often without much form to guide them towards a decision. I flatter myself that I have proved a pretty reliable runner, over the years!'

There was something disconcertingly confident about this fellow, thought Lambert. If he was their murderer, he was doing an excellent job of presenting a man without a care in the world. National institution Sir Bradley Morton might be, but was he really as good an actor as that?

Lambert said brusquely, 'Your resentment of people who make money from drama without ever appearing on stage or on television sets doesn't extend to authors, though, if I remember rightly.'

Brad looked baffled for an instant before his face brightened. 'Ah, you are recalling the conversation we had yesterday, when I expressed my enthusiasm about Dennis Potter to you! Because I come from these parts, Dennis is rather a special case for me. We both walked the Forest of Dean in our youth, though I was younger than Dennis and didn't know him then. I reiterate that in my view Potter remains our greatest television playwright. But authors aren't like angels; many of them began as actors. And they give us our very lifeblood.'

The old knight was enjoying this link with high culture and he warmed to his theme. 'Authors write the lines we speak on stage or screen, and no actor can survive a bad script. We live or die by the words we speak, and the people who provide them for us make a unique contribution to British culture. I was much praised for my Falstaff, but it was the Bard's ability to encapsulate humanity in all its many shades which gave me the opportunity to sway the house.'

In his spare time, Lambert was a fair golfer, who had insisted on introducing Hook to that infuriating game when he had relinquished cricket. He now noted certain parallels between ageing golfers and ageing theatrical knights. Golfers always remembered the very best of their athletic youth and forgot their deficiencies. He had a shrewd idea that Sir Bradley Morton's Falstaff had brought mixed reviews, but Sir Bradley spoke of it with a majestic recall, as if his caperings in the Boar's Head tavern could be set beside the greatest fat knights of the twentieth century. Actors, like golfers, like humanity in general perhaps, bathed reality in the golden glow of remembrance.

Lambert said, 'You were pressing Samuel Jackson for more work.'

'That was some time ago. Circumstances have changed.' Bradley wondered whether to tell them that his days were limited, that future work was no longer an issue. But he felt that clutching the knowledge to himself gave him a kind of dignity. Death was the ultimate trump card, to which there was no reply. He would keep that card up his sleeve for the moment. It gave him a feeling of superiority, of standing aside from these men and their necessary but sordid investigation. He hadn't even told Sandra Rokeby about the terminal nature of his case, when she had been good enough to run him to the hospital this morning. He wondered how much that shrewd woman had gathered of his situation and his activities. Sandra had always been considerably more than the collection of curves she presented to the popular press.

Lambert was studying him closely and disconcertingly, as he did all of his interviewees. 'Sir Bradley, you told us yesterday that Samuel Jackson was a friend of yours and that you had a high regard for him. Other people have told us a different story. Would you now care to revise your account of your relationship?'

'Yes. I was being over-sentimental.'

'Or dishonest.'

Sir Bradley Morton looked for a moment outraged. Then he forced himself to relax into a smile. 'That's how it looks to you. I can see that. Could we settle for both sentimental and dishonest? They often go together, I suppose – perhaps more so for actors than for others. I'd known Sam Jackson since he was a young man, but I don't suppose I liked him any more than did others in the cast.'

'By all accounts he wasn't a likeable man. But that doesn't mean that you should attempt to deceive us about your relationship with him. Why did you do that?'

The knight wasn't used to being challenged like this. People joked with him, flattered him, were disproportionately pleased by his small jokes. But basically they deferred to him and he had grown used to deference. Challenge was a novelty and he was rusty when it came to coping with it. 'I suppose I was unnerved. I was being questioned about a murder. I hadn't met that situation before. Not many people have, and you must accept that we are disturbed by it. My reaction was defensive. I wanted to clear myself of any involvement in Sam's death. I suppose I thought that if you accepted I was a friend of his, you would think I was unlikely to have killed him. So I pretended we had been closer over the years than we had.'

'And now that has been exposed as deceit. That deceit must make you more of a suspect for these crimes.'

Brad gave them a serene smile. When your lungs had delivered a death sentence to you, police suspicion scarcely mattered. But he determined again not to tell them about that. That would be the secret he retained, the secret which would preserve his feeling of superiority to all this questioning, which would allow him to view these queries as the pettiness they were for him. 'I'm now quite prepared to admit that I didn't like Sam Jackson any more than anyone else did. In my view, indeed, the world is a better place without him. That doesn't mean that I killed him though, does it?'

Lambert ignored the question and pressed on hard with this over-verbose man who seemed almost unaware that he was a suspect for two murders. 'Ernest Clark possessed all the information which Jackson had been using to coerce his cast members. We think he proposed to use it in the same way: in effect, to blackmail cast members in the Inspector Loxton series to accept pay and conditions which they would not otherwise have entertained. In your case, he probably proposed to deny you further work in subsequent series.'

Sir Bradley bathed them in that superior, knowing, exasperating smile. If only you knew, he thought. But you shan't know. This is my secret and my advantage. 'These things would have been subject to negotiation, as they always are. I should have weighed whatever Ernie had to offer against the wealth of opportunities available to me elsewhere. Then I should have made a rational decision.'

'You are still receiving plenty of other offers, are you, Sir

Bradley? Forgive the impertinence of the enquiry, but you will see that it has a bearing on how important any decision of Mr Clark's might have been to you.'

He was very tempted to tell them that he had shot his last location scene today, that a couple of short scenes in the studio would conclude a long and varied acting life. But his resolution to keep his secret held. He felt for a moment as if he were looking down on these men from a great height and seeing their enquiries into his conduct as the trivialities they were. He said almost impishly, 'I didn't kill Ernie Clark. I wonder who on earth did?'

'Someone almost certainly asked him to drive to your hotel last night. Someone met him and talked with him at the end of the hotel car park. Someone put a bullet through his head and left him to die there.'

'You make it all sound very dramatic. I should appreciate that, as an actor. But all I want you to do really is to arrest someone for this. My curiosity is aroused and I wonder who that could be. The fact that it now seems even more likely to be one of my acting colleagues who dispatched our two financiers and producers makes it only more intriguing.'

'It wasn't you who arranged for Clark to come?'

'It quite certainly wasn't me.'

'And you didn't sit in his Jaguar and discuss the future with him?'

'No, I did not.' He was tempted again to tell them that he had no future to discuss, and again that strange feeling of superiority infused him as he held his peace.

'You have more experience of life, of the theatre, and of most of your fellow-professionals involved in this than anyone else. We have questioned people thoroughly, but you may still know things which we do not about some of them. It is my belief that you have a shrewd idea who killed these two men, whether or not you have the evidence available to support that idea. Presumably I do not need to remind you that it is your citizen's duty to inform us of any thoughts you have about a culprit. What you say here will prove confidential, if it proves to be mistaken.'

Morton looked from one to the other of the two very different but equally expectant faces and it seemed for a moment that he would do as they suggested. Then he shook his head abruptly. 'I don't know, I'm afraid. It's nice of you to credit me with such knowledge, but I really know much less about the private lives of the rest of the cast than you assume I do.'

Hook, who had done nothing save observe him so far, now spoke softly. 'Sam Jackson was not a very fit man. We think whoever strangled him with his necktie took him completely by surprise and killed him very quickly. Ernie Clark was shot through the temple with a pistol; again he appears to have been taken by surprise and offered little resistance. This means that both of these crimes could have been committed by a woman. Have you any thoughts on that and on the women involved in the case?'

Brad's smile turned almost to a nervous giggle in his relief. 'For a moment, DS Hook, I thought that you were about to suggest that it would have been perfectly possible for a man of my advanced years to have committed these crimes. I thought indeed that you were about to make some sort of accusation, or at least some sort of villainous suggestion! Curiously enough, I find that thought flattering rather than scandalous. The theory that I might even in the twilight of my career have rid the world of television drama of two of its more repellent men seems to hint at the virility and judgement still within this ageing frame rather than at any vicious evil lurking deep within me.'

Hook caught a flash of Lambert's impatience at the old man's garrulity. He said rather less gently, 'The women in the cast, Sir Bradley. Do you think one of them might be responsible for these murders?'

'Now that I come to think of it, I have to confess that I have not previously entertained either of the women with major roles in the Inspector Loxton series as candidates for these crimes. Old-fashioned and unrealistic chivalry, I suppose you'd call that. I expect you see quite enough viciousness on the distaff side of our species to include women from the outset as candidates for serious crimes. Well, let's try to give proper consideration to your question, shall we? I've known Sandra Rokeby for many years now.'

'And she had known both of our victims for many years, Sir Bradley.'

'Indeed. Long enough to build up a considerable enmity, I think you are suggesting. Well, Sandra is no angel; nor would she claim to be one.' He smiled as some libidinous memory struck him, but did not enlighten them.

'Sandra had reasons to dislike Sam, even to hate him. He knew things about her that very few other people knew. Highly embarrassing things, which he used to control her.'

If Morton knew about the porn film, he didn't mention it. 'He knew things about all of us and used them against all of us, which is what made him such a thoroughly unpleasant man. Sandra is much more than an ageing Page Three pin-up. I count her as a friend and I certainly shouldn't like to have her as an opponent. She'd be much more formidable than her popular image indicates she would. But I can't see her as a murderess, whatever embarrassments Sam threatened her with. No way.'

This was a much more thoughtful and astute man than the amiable image of the national treasure he had previously presented. Hook fancied that he was enjoying presenting this other and more subtle side of himself. He even persuaded himself that he would value the man's opinions. 'What about Peg Reynolds?'

'I don't know her anything like as well as Sandra. I'll tell you one thing, though: Peg's going to be a hell of an actress. Long after I've left this earth, Peg Reynolds will be dominating stages and screens. It's an uncertain business, ours, but unless she has health problems or makes serious enemies among the hierarchy, she'll become a household name within the next generation. But that isn't what you asked me, is it? You're interested in her as a potential murderer. I'd prefer to bill that crazy boyfriend of hers as a candidate, because I could quite see him doing something violent, under stress. But we know that he has a cast-iron alibi for Sam's murder, because he wasn't even around at the time, and the two deaths must surely be connected.'

'And Miss Reynolds?'

'I've got to beware of the charms of a very pretty face on

the most promising actress I've seen in years. I can't envisage Peg twisting that tie round Sam's neck or turning a pistol upon Ernie, but I'm forced to admit it's just possible. I think that young lady is cool enough and organized enough to commit these crimes, if she had a reason to do so. And it seems everyone around Sam Jackson had a reason to do so. He gave us all reasons to hate him, almost as if it were one of his missions in life.'

'That is an interesting view, and we know that Miss Reynolds is also under stress from other sources. Stress leads often to rash actions.'

'Indeed. I've seen severe bruising on Peg Reynolds' upper arms and back, when we've been changing or adjusting costumes. That had nothing to do with Sam, but I've seen people suffering that sort of physical violence lash out at other people indiscriminately. It seems quite preposterous that anyone like Peg Reynolds could have done these things, but then it seems almost equally preposterous that any of the men should be involved in this.'

Hook glanced at Lambert, who said, 'Thank you for volunteering your thoughts to us. You know more of the personalities of the people we are considering than we do, even after detailed police questioning. Please go on thinking about this and make us aware of any new thoughts you have on these deaths.'

They discussed him, of course, when he had gone, agreeing that he had greater and more thoughtful depths than they had previously suspected. At length Lambert said, 'He seemed very frank with us today. But he still had the air of knowing something important which we didn't know, which gave him a sort of effortless superiority.'

Sir Bradley Morton was by this time well on the way back to the hotel, forcing himself once again to confront the notion of early and inescapable death, which had been with him all day. It took a man time to accept these things, but he'd had plenty of time now. And the acceptance of the inevitable, once achieved, brought with it a sort of composure.

David Deeney arrived at the café by the river in Ross-on-Wye two minutes in advance of the time he had specified, but Trevor

Fisher was already there, looking anxiously towards the road above him where he knew David would have to park. He was like a worried child, thought Deeney, with the impatience which he had told himself on the way here that he would not feel.

'I waited for you to come before I ordered,' said Trevor. 'You can assemble a full afternoon tea here, if you wish to. I'm going to have scones and cakes and lots of tea.' He liked the old-fashioned full afternoon tea which was now quite rare, with bread and butter and jam and a variety of cakes. Childish, David thought irritably, though he had always previously rejoiced in the innocent enjoyment of his partner in such things. 'I'd better confine myself to a cup of tea. I'll have to eat a full dinner with the others this evening. Perhaps I'll steal half a scone from you, if you feel you can spare it.'

The river flowed softly here, wide and unthreatening. A hundred yards below them, dogs barked excitedly and swam swiftly after sticks. The shrill shouts and laughter of excited children echoed as they played on the wide stretch of green beside the water. David thought of that other stretch of the Wye, beside the hotel where he had stayed for the last week, equally picturesque but very different from this. There the river flowed softly below them in a deep cleft, its beauty part of a wider scene in which fields ran away to slopes and eventually to mountains in the west. It seemed in his imagination a more sinister beauty now, because it was identified with the killing which had so recently taken place beside it.

'I thought you'd originally planned to come home tonight,' said Trevor. He bit fiercely into a scone, as though to divert himself.

David thought that sounded like an accusation, a tedious wife's complaint about the fracturing of the domestic idyll. He must be under more strain from the week's events than he had thought. 'The police want us to stay on. They're still investigating these crimes. They don't tell you much, but I get the impression they haven't made much progress so far.' He tried not to sound over-pleased about that. Trevor was bound to pick him up if he got the notion that David was glad that the police were baffled. Tact wasn't Trevor Fisher's strong point. Deeney tried to feel affectionate rather than displeased by that.

'Will you be home tomorrow night?' Trevor asked ingenuously.

'I don't know yet, do I? The police will tell us when we can leave the scene of the crime.'

In fact, they would probably have allowed him to go home, even tonight, as he lived only in Oxford and could be readily available to them there. But he didn't wish to leave the group. There was an obscure feeling of safety in numbers and he needed to know what was going on as far as others' dealings with the police were concerned. He said gruffly, 'I'll let you know what's going on. I'll give you a ring tomorrow, if there's anything to report.'

Trevor buttered and jammed the top half of a scone meticulously, then slid it on to his companion's plate. He looked past David towards the river and the distant bridge downstream. 'Who do you think killed these people?'

He was like a child picking at a sore, David thought irritably; he couldn't bear to leave alone a matter which his companion had made plain he did not want to discuss. He knew that was unfair: it was only natural that his partner would want to talk about the sensational events of the last few days, especially when his normal life was so humdrum. He was being oversensitive. But Trevor should have expected that, after he'd so stupidly told the police about how his partner had disposed of his 'almost new' trainers in odd circumstances. Surely he should see that the proper course now was to keep off the subject of murder and discuss something safer and more anodyne. David said evenly, 'I've no idea who killed Sam and Ernie. That's police business and they're getting on with it at this moment, I expect.'

'That's rather a thrilling thought, isn't it? I'd have thought you'd be intrigued to know who'd killed the two of them – especially if it's someone you've worked with every day over the last few weeks.'

That was a fair point, of course. They had all been looking at each other speculatively across the dinner table on the last few nights, apart from Peg Reynolds and James Turner, who seemed to find their own problems even more pressing. David Deeney took a deep breath and addressed himself to the problems of his own relationship. 'You're right. I'm sure each of us is making all sorts of wild hypotheses. It's a relief when we have to think intensely about our acting. You have to concentrate to do that and you have to be aware of others and work with them. It's been a positive relief to have location scenes to concentrate on this week.'

'Yes. I think I can see that, even though I've never acted myself.' Trevor Fisher looked past his lover again, to where the smooth surface of the river was broken by a slowly cruising swan. 'If you'd killed these people, you know, I'd understand. Sam Jackson was horrible to you. If he'd said something unforgivable and you just couldn't bear it, so that you lost your temper completely. I'd stick by you.'

The swan was drifting downriver now, close to his mate and seemingly oblivious of all else.

SEVENTEEN

John Lambert went out into his garden to inspect the spring blossom on his flowering cherries and the promising buds which were massing on his rose trees. It was his normal way of switching off at the end of a week, of announcing to himself as much as to others that Chief Superintendent Lambert was to be set aside in favour of John Lambert, husband, father and grandfather.

Christine watched him through the window as he appeared and disappeared amongst the shrubs and trees. He was looking older; there could now be no doubt about that. The tall man's slight stoop was a little more pronounced; the determined adoption of an upright position took a little longer than it had done a few years ago because of the stiffness which was invading the tall frame. It was to be expected, but that didn't make it any more agreeable to her.

There was no use repeating the conversation they had undertaken several times over the last year about retirement; it was one of the issues on which they had agreed to disagree. He wouldn't welcome it, it would lead nowhere, and both of them would be irritated and dissatisfied. Much better to let the suggestion of weariness and retirement come from John himself, but he was as usual stubbornly recalcitrant about such things.

Christine knew her man, which meant that she knew also that he wasn't going to be able to switch off for the weekend on this Friday night. The headlines about what the press had elected to call the 'Herefordshire Horrors Murders' had grown larger and blacker as the week progressed. Radio and television had all sorts of shots of the familiar principals of the Inspector Loxton series to sustain interest, which had been renewed and increased with the second murder on Thursday. Even the man who had made a reputation as the 'Super Sleuth' was baffled by the week's sensational happenings, the media trumpeted with satisfaction.

'Any progress?' she asked tentatively as John came back into the kitchen. He would expect her to ask, but too much media attention always made him tetchy.

He made himself stop and be polite, knowing that Christine meant well. As a young, thrusting CID man, he had shut her out of his working life, refusing to comment at all on cases, preferring indeed that she had no idea what he was doing. She had guided their two girls through their infancy with very little assistance from John, who had rarely been around when it mattered. Younger officers saw the Lamberts' marriage as rock-like, but Christine alone knew how near it had come to foundering in those early years. 'They're a funny lot, these actors and directors,' said John. It was the nearest he could get to an affectionate rejoinder.

'Aren't they affected by the thought that someone in their midst, someone they know and perhaps like, has killed two people?'

'I suppose they are. But that's what I mean when I say they're a funny lot. When they're acting, they seem to be able to switch off all other emotions and just concentrate upon the matter in hand. I've heard them actually congratulating themselves on what they've achieved this week. It's almost as if two murders in their midst are a secondary consideration.'

'They're lucky, I suppose, being professionally engaged in something which demands absolute concentration, with no room for anything else.'

'I suppose so. But it's no help to people like Bert Hook and me. We need their full attention on two killings.' He sat down at the table and sighed, shaking his head at the pans on the hob and the signs of busy, innocent domesticity. 'I've felt all day that we're very near a solution, that I'm missing something which is staring me in the face. But so far the penny hasn't dropped.'

'You're tired, John. Have a decent meal and watch a bit of television. Switching off completely is often the prelude to something striking you which has escaped you until then.'

She was the rock of common sense which every senior copper needed. It had taken him far too long to realize that, he thought. 'I smell curry, which I shall enjoy, as always! And you shall select the television programmes for the evening. I shall avoid all executive decisions.'

It was light-hearted and conciliatory, an acknowledgement he did not make often enough of how important she was to him. He did not realize at that moment how important a decision it would prove to be.

Peg Reynolds found a very different James Turner when she got back to the hotel. After his attitude over the last few days, she had been dreading confronting him, wondering indeed when and how she could end the whole messy and painful affair.

'A man called Datchet has been in touch from the Coventry Playhouse. He wanted to know if you'd be available to play St Joan.' James sounded exultant, almost boastful to impart such exciting news.

'At Coventry? That's brilliant! I hope you didn't sound too eager.'

She felt suddenly guilty that she had been contacted about this whilst James had nothing, but he was more enthusiastic than she had seen him in many weeks. 'I knew you hadn't an agent at the moment, so I took over. I told him you'd other possibilities on the table and that you would need a definite offer before you could even consider it.'

'James! If you try to be cavalier with them, they'll offer it to someone else. Everyone wants to play the Maid.'

'It's all right. He's been back to me three times during the day. It's now a definite offer and the money's been doubled since the first figure was named. Half an hour ago, I secured you the right of veto over who is going to play Warwick, Cauchon and the Dauphin. In effect, you can almost cast the important parts yourself.'

'James, you shouldn't joke about things like this! It's too important for jokes.'

'No jokes, darling. This is absolutely serious. I really think I might be rather good at it. Bloody sight better than I am at acting, with any luck. But you've got a definite offer, at a salary which is four times anything you've earned before for stage work. They're putting it in writing and you should have it by Monday at the latest.'

He was a transformed creature from the tortured individual

she had left that morning. His eyes shone and he had a bright, excited smile. 'I think I might have actually discovered something in this agent business. The lines all came quite naturally to me and I thoroughly enjoyed delivering them. Of course, I was conscious that I had something very desirable to sell, so I made the most of that.'

'I can't believe it!'

'You'll have the evidence in writing in the next day or two. Possibly tomorrow morning. I think we should celebrate, don't you?'

He took her to bed and it was like the early days, the ones which had made her lose her head over him. He was tender and gentle at first, then more vigorous and forceful when she demanded it and her body arched urgently backwards beneath him. It was a long time since he had been so relaxed and so attentive to her needs.

They showered and dressed slowly, as if to prolong the atmosphere between them. It was James who said, 'I think we should eat with the others tonight. It might be our last night together. That's if they'll have me – I know I haven't behaved very well towards them.'

'They're rather protective of me, that's all.' She could have bitten her tongue off. It wasn't a tactful thing to say, and tact had been very necessary with James Turner over the last month or two.

But he didn't react badly. He nodded ruefully and said, 'You need your friends and I've kept you away from them. I've got reparations to make. I know that.' He reached up and held her softly against him, stroking the bruises on her back and at the top of her arms with an exquisite tenderness. People said the violent leopard never changed his spots, but she felt now that there was hope. She said softly, 'Some of the people who left RADA at the same time as me still haven't got agents. I could let you know which ones I think are really talented and will eventually make their way in the profession. They wouldn't bring much to you at the moment, but I think three or four of them have great potential.'

'Thank you. You never know: perhaps all they need is a really good, really energetic agent!'

She was proud to go down with him to dinner. He looked even more handsome than usual, Peg thought, now that he was relaxed.

Turner got a muted welcome from the other woman in the party. Sandra Rokeby had experienced all sorts of men in her time and the violent ones were the worst. He had a long way to go to earn real forgiveness, in her view. Meantime she would give him the benefit of the doubt and merely watch his conduct with Peg Reynolds carefully. At least he wasn't a candidate for murderer; he'd been miles away when Sam Jackson had been strangled. Sandra was almost regretful about that. But then who was there around this increasingly noisy table whom one could entertain seriously as a killer?

Martin Buttivant? She wondered if you always thought of the leading man in a television series as the likeliest candidate. Was that sexist? Was it theatrical? Probably – the idea that an actor playing a leading part was somehow more likely to kill than someone in a small role must surely be stupid, mustn't it? She glanced across at Martin who was in animated conversation with John Watts. She was admiring his Savile Row suit when she caught his keen blue eyes for a moment and reflected on how far he had come since they had both been desperate enough to leap between those off-white sheets and into that stupid porn movie all those years ago.

Martin had certainly moved on a long way since then. Playing Ben Loxton in this series had been the making of him as an actor and even more as a big earner. Martin would have lost more than anyone if Sam Jackson or Ernie Clark had blown the gaffe on him. But the idea of him as a ruthless killer still seemed ridiculous. Perhaps you could never entertain the idea of a lover as murderer, even though it was all those years ago since their relationship.

John Watts was perhaps the person at the table who looked most like a murderer. Sandra allowed herself a small, private smile at that ridiculous concept. What on earth was a murderer supposed to look like? Like Crippen? Like the Yorkshire Ripper? Like the notorious Fred West, who had operated in these parts for twenty years? John Watts had a thin face, very deep-set eyes, and a small beard which tended to wag frantically when he spoke. Why did that look like a murderer's physiognomy to her? Didn't that say more about her than about John Watts?

Still, even if you discounted his appearance entirely, John had some of the qualifications for the perpetrator of these crimes. He was very able – probably in the general sense of coping with life and its challenges he was the most capable person at the table. They'd lost both their producers this week, and producers were in one sense the most vital people of all in any theatrical enterprise, because they provided the money and the resources and the organization which got it off the ground and then kept it moving.

Yet John Watts had made the transition from a serene past with the secure backing of his producers to an uncertain future with scarcely a tremor. He had been responsible for the direction of the Ben Loxton series from the start, but he had now added a much wider dimension of responsibility. Already finances and support for the future had been ensured, with Richard Aitchison enlisted to finance them. Watts was going to make more money and become more of a television entrepreneur himself: the others said he was going to do very well out of the new arrangements.

Yet that was surely fair enough, wasn't it? He'd stepped in and sorted things out in the crisis, as no one else had had the skills and the knowledge to do. The translation from the egregious Sam Jackson to the new regime had been almost seamless. Almost as if John Watts had known that it was coming, in fact. Sandra tried not to dwell upon that thought.

She glanced reflectively at Sir Bradley Morton, whom she had taken to hospital that morning. He was such a lovable old fraud most of the time that you couldn't be certain how ill he really was. He was certainly looking older, but when you were well into your seventies and at the end of a week's location filming that was only to be expected. He'd been quiet on the way back from the hospital and she'd thought at one stage that he was on the point of confiding the details of his illness to her. Perhaps it was something like prostate trouble which he didn't want to talk about because of its sexual connotations. When you had a reputation as a lively old roué with a history of conquests and a reputation for easy success with females, you didn't want to talk about things like that, she supposed.

It surely couldn't be Brad who'd seen off Sam and Ernie, could it? National institutions didn't go around killing people. And Sir Bradley Morton had less to fear than anyone from whatever revelations Sam Jackson or Ernie Clark might make about him. When you were a national treasure, you were almost unassailable. The person who made any unwelcome revelation was more likely to be assailed than you were, for daring to sully your image. Sir Bradley Morton must be almost scandal-proof by now.

David Deeney must be a possibility for these crimes, she told herself. He was a quiet man, though a highly competent actor – not a common combination, that! Sam Jackson had probably been more horrible to him than to anyone here, principally on account of his being openly gay. That was common enough among actors, God knows, but Sam had affected to take a particular exception to David, perhaps because he was quiet and self-effacing. But quiet people like anyone else can be driven beyond the bounds of endurance. Perhaps Sam had said something or made some threat to Deeney which had been the last straw and caused him to erupt into violence. It seemed at least as likely as any other of the highly unlikely possibilities which presented themselves to her around this convivial table.

That was a fair word to describe it. The noise level was rising steadily and there were more bursts of laughter around the table as the meal proceeded. Peg Reynolds was radiant tonight. Her always impressive black hair looked even more lustrous with the dining-room lighting immediately behind her; her large brown eyes seemed wider than ever as they glittered with pleasure. The femme fatale who had despatched the villainous Sam Jackson? A cliché which seemed less likely as she saw how happy and unstrained Peg looked tonight. Her torments had come from a different quarter than Jackson or Clark. James Turner had been her torturer, but tonight the pair seemed at least for the moment to have resolved all that.

They were almost opposite Sandra and she could hear most

of their conversation. Turner was reassuring Peg: 'You can rely on getting Saint Joan, really you can. It's a matter of when, and how much they pay you, not if.' He turned to David Deeney on his right. 'Would you be interested in playing Warwick if the part were to be offered to you?'

It was bold, even impertinent, Sandra thought. But there was reason in it. Deeney was a highly capable actor. His Warwick would be quiet but menacing, an obvious danger to Joan even in the scenes where her enthusiasm carried her forward and made her seem more than mortal.

David said, 'I would be interested, were it ever to come to fruition. I should point out that I already have an agent with whom I am well satisfied.'

'That's no problem,' said James brightly. 'I wouldn't be looking for any profit from the casting of Warwick. It's simply that I want Peg as my client to be surrounded with the best possible players and I think that your experience and ability would be of great help to her.'

Deeney looked at him for a moment, then turned and beamed unexpectedly upon Peg Reynolds. 'He might go far as an agent, this man. He already has all the right talk.'

It was spoken light-heartedly and Turner knew it. But he said earnestly, 'Do you know, I think you might be right? I think I might be much better at representing good actors than trying to be one myself! I've already had three important phone conversations and I have to say I positively enjoyed myself. Maybe I've found my natural metier at last!' He grinned at Deeney and then at Peg, who looked both delighted and relieved.

It was John Watts, fulfilling his function as the unofficial factotum of the company, who spoke from four places away down the table. 'Good for you, James! I speak as a failed actor myself. I was struggling in bit parts for a couple of years before someone gave me my chance as a director. I wondered constantly why small parts didn't lead in turn to bigger ones, but the truth was that I simply wasn't good enough. It's not easy to be objective about oneself and the effects one is making, and least of all in acting. If you're an accountant, I presume you get things right or wrong and the evidence stares up at you on paper. When you're on stage, it's such a nervy business and everyone is so much on edge about their own performance that they tell you you're marvellous, even if you're crap. Eventually, I saw the rushes of a little scene I'd done for telly and realized I was rubbish. I think it was something in which Sir Bradley was starring, actually!'

Morton smiled at him graciously. 'I don't remember, John. It was no doubt a long time ago, because you've been known as a highly successful director for at least twenty years. So the stage lost an indifferent actor and gained an imaginative and sensitive director, from which actors have benefited ever since. These things work themselves out, if we allow them to.'

It was perhaps too glib a cliché to stand up to close examination, but it was the sort of thing they all wanted to hear. Despite the sensational crimes which beset them still, this was after all the conclusion of a successful week of location shooting, and they were allowed to be sentimental and affectionate towards each other. They drank freely as the laughter rose higher, but not as much as they would have expected. There was the pleasant fatigue which follows high tension, and each of them was reluctant to be the one who broke up the company.

They did not go out and walk by the river, as many of them had intended to do. Their warm lethargy kept them tonight in the lounge, where the laughter and the ancient theatrical reminiscences continued. They didn't see the trophy retrieved from the Wye by the policeman-angler and the frogman-angler whom Bert Hook had recruited earlier in the day. It was a clear, sunlit evening and the twilight lasted for a long time. But the light was fading fast when they lifted their trophy from a shallow pool where the river turned gently towards the west.

The pistol which had ended the life of Ernest Clark gleamed softly in the near-darkness.

Back in the bungalow which was his haven, John Lambert set the remote control firmly into Christine's hands and demanded that she make the television decisions.

The decision was in fact quite easy – probably the one John would have made for himself had he been in control. Several nights earlier, they had recorded a BBC documentary about Melvyn Bragg. John was an admirer as she was of the Cumbrian polymath. They had been looking forward to watching this together. It wasn't disappointing. It was the kind of thing the BBC did well and American television would never have ventured upon, said John after twenty minutes.

They went through Bragg's early life as a humble working-class boy and his gaining entry to the grammar school. As always, there was a teacher who had been a particular inspiration. Melvyn was generous about his influence and his work with the brighter sixth-form boys, and the programme dug him out as an alert ninety-three-year-old and united him with his former protégé. Bragg was lively as always and as Labour peer in the House of Lords, contrived effortlessly to insult both Eton and its latest Conservative prime minister.

It was an item towards the end of the documentary which made John Lambert ease himself softly forward on to the edge of his seat and become full of rapt attention. He sat very still for five minutes when the recording had finished, then rang Bert Hook. His sergeant had seen the programme when it was first broadcast several days previously, but he had not made the connection his chief had made with the key item in it.

It was well after ten now, but the pair spent twelve minutes in earnest exchanges before Lambert said almost as an afterthought, 'Your men found what I'm certain will prove to be the weapon which murdered Ernie Clark, by the way. They came up with a pistol in the Wye, almost exactly opposite the spot in the car park where Clark died. The station rang me an hour or so ago.'

'Do you think we'll get a confession?'

'I don't know. These actors operate in a different world from yours and mine. I'll pick you up at around a quarter to nine.'

EIGHTEEN

Lambert drove slowly through the lanes of Herefordshire, which were heavy with the bright green of new leaves. He was giving himself time to think. As he'd said to Hook last night, he wasn't used to actors and he wasn't sure of the best tactics to adopt with this one.

Sir Bradley Morton was standing by the desk in the reception area of the hotel, perusing a copy of *The Times*. He greeted them affably. When they said that this needed somewhere private, he suggested immediately that they should retire to his room. 'We shall all be moving out today, I expect,' he said as they mounted the stairs. 'It's a relief to have this week over.' It wasn't clear whether he was referring to the location filming or to the dramatic deaths on Tuesday and Thursday of the week. Strange lot, these actors, Lambert told himself once again.

Sir Bradley had the best accommodation in the hotel, as befitted a well-loved national treasure. It was a suite rather than a single bedroom, the spacious main room had a king-size double bed, a large wardrobe, a chest of drawers, and two armchairs. There was a small dressing room between the bedroom and the spacious en suite bathroom beyond it.

'I didn't ask for this,' said Morton, almost apologetically. 'I think it's supposed to be the bridal suite. I was simply allotted it amongst the accommodation which had been booked for the company. I suppose having a title helps. The British are still very class conscious, aren't they, and hotels more than anyone?' He set his visitors comfortably in the two armchairs and perched himself on the edge of the bed to face them. 'And what can I do to help the long arm of the law today?'

'You went to hospital in Gloucester yesterday. You were driven there by Miss Rokeby, I believe. Could you tell us the nature of your illness, please?'

His bonhomie faded. 'That is private. If I choose to keep the details to myself, that is surely my business.'

'Not if it has any sort of bearing upon events earlier in the week.' Lambert's tone was as uncompromising as his expression.

Morton glared at him, tried to stare him down, and failed. He dropped his eyes to the carpet, focussed on a wisp of cotton which must have fallen from the bed, allowed the silence to stretch whilst he thought. 'I don't suppose it matters. I was going to tell the others when it was time for us to break up and go our separate ways. I planned to tell them today that I wouldn't be working with them again and thank them for what we've had together – what they've given to me and what I hope I've given to them.'

'You were going to tell them this morning that your illness was terminal?'

Lambert seemed to know and Brad decided that made it easier. They knew all sorts of things, these coppers, and this John Lambert seemed to know more than most. 'I was going to tell them that I expect to be dead in six weeks, two months at the outside. That somehow seems more dramatic than terminal. We actors like to be dramatic, whenever we can. You may have noticed that.'

'When did you decide to kill Sam Jackson?'

The detective was making it easier for him with his knowledge, with his assumption that they both knew all about this. But Brad answered him with another question: 'What was it that made you suspect me? I've less obvious motive than most of the others.'

'You told me five minutes into our first meeting how much you admired Dennis Potter as a television playwright.'

'Ah, vanity, you see. The actor's besetting sin. I have an image as a chaser of skirts and a leerer at camera lenses and I wanted to be associated with something more worthy and intellectual and challenging. "Vanity of vanities; all is vanity," as the Good Book tells us. Dennis was born in the village of Berry Hill in the Forest of Dean, you know. I was born within ten miles of there, a year or two later than him. We both endured bible quotations at least twice on Sundays, when we were children.'

'But you had more personal connections than that. You appeared in some of his plays, as you told us on Thursday.' He wanted suddenly to be generous to this peacockish, mistaken, dying man.

'Yes. I was in *Vote, Vote, Vote for Nigel Barton* back in 1965. I was only a lad then, taking my first steps in acting. And I was in *Pennies from Heaven* in 1978. Only bit parts, mind you, both times. You'd hardly have noticed me if you hadn't been vigilant. My mum was vigilant; she was still alive then.' Death had strange effects, he thought. It was making him both honest and modest, two of the things he had long since forgotten in his acting and public personas.

'It was your mention of Potter which connected you with this week's deaths. Not until last night, unfortunately.'

The old knight frowned. 'Why then?' He wasn't going to argue his innocence – there was no point, with the grim reaper waiting in the wings.

Lambert smiled sadly. 'My wife played me a recording she'd made of a BBC programme. A documentary about Melvyn Bragg. I don't know when it was first broadcast.'

'They tried to get him to interview me once, you know. Just after I'd been knighted, I think. My people thought it would be good for me to appear with an intellectual heavyweight and his people thought – well, I don't quite know what they thought. Perhaps that it would be good for Melvyn to be seen slumming it with popular culture. Anyway, it never came off. "Pressure of commitments" both sides said. That's what they always say when they don't want to reveal the truth.'

This was the most curious unmasking of a killer John Lambert had ever undertaken. He said almost reluctantly, 'There was a brief extract from Bragg's interview with the dying Dennis Potter in the programme I saw last night. It was when he was in the grip of cancer and had to take swigs of morphine juice.'

'I remember. I expect I shall get to that stage, eventually.' He spoke as if that would satisfy some of his curiosity about the process of death. 'That was a magnificent last outburst from Dennis. The dying of the light. He did not go gentle into that good night.'

'Indeed he didn't. Unfortunately, I remembered some of the things he said. And one in particular.'

'Did you really? It's never been rebroadcast in its entirety, that interview, which is a great pity, in my view.'

'You obviously recall it very well, Brad.' It was the first time he had used the old actor's first name: an acknowledgement that the normal formalities of police interviewing had gone for ever now for Morton. 'Dennis Potter said that impending death absolved you of the consequences of your actions. He said that he would like to kill someone, because of what he considered his baleful influence on the media. No one took him seriously, because he was far too ill by then to make the journey and take the steps to kill anyone.'

'Rupert Murdoch.'

'That's whom Dennis had singled out for dispatch, yes. The victim scarcely matters. It was the idea of being able to kill someone without retribution when you are under a natural sentence of death yourself which interested you – and which now has to interest me.'

'It's quite an attractive option, don't you think? But then I don't suppose you'd feel qualified to comment, not having experienced the situation for yourself.'

'You decided that you would rid the world of Sam Jackson.'

'I decided that he was my equivalent of what Murdoch was for Dennis. I have a narrower perspective than Dennis Potter, as befits my inferior intellect. But I could offer a great service to my fellow actors, many of whom I had grown to love, by removing that vile man from their presence and from the world's presence.'

'You should tell us now how you did it, Brad, to complete the formalities.'

'It was surprisingly easy, you know. I walked into that caravan of his on Tuesday and waited for him to insult me or threaten me. It took him about thirty seconds to do both. He didn't realize that I was near death and therefore unassailable. He'd left his tie conveniently loose for me, almost as if he was a willing accessory to the deed. I freed the knot and twisted both ends vigorously, more vigorously than I would ever have thought possible. I think he must have been almost dead before he even realized what I was about.'

'Why did you kill him, Brad? What had you to gain by having him dead?'

Sir Bradley Morton smiled benignly, first at Lambert and then at Hook, as if they were merely inviting him to state the obvious. 'I was rendering a public service. Surely you can see that? Just the same as Dennis Potter felt he would have been, if he could have got at his target.'

'But Potter recognized even as he stated the idea that he couldn't possibly reach his target, didn't he? There was something rather impish about it, as I remember it.'

'Maybe. That means I was much luckier, then, doesn't it? My target was accessible. And the world is much better off without Jackson, isn't it? Have you heard one person regret his death?'

There was little point in discussing ethics or morality with this bright-eyed, confident man. 'There would be anarchy if no one respected the law, Brad.'

'But most people do. For most of their lives, they have to. Only a tiny minority are in a position to behave as I have done. If every person who knows that he is about to die took out one villain, the world would be a better place.'

'We cannot allow people to make arbitrary decisions about who deserves to be eliminated and who should survive.'

'Maybe not. Maybe not everyone is as clear-sighted as I was. Maybe not everyone will have as unequivocal a villain as Sam Jackson to attack.'

'But violence leads to more violence. We see it all the time, in our work. You went on to kill Ernie Clark.'

'Yes. I hadn't envisaged that at all. But Ernie brought it upon himself.'

The old killer's mantra. The absence of any hint of conscience as one crime led on to another. 'You contacted him – arranged to meet him in the car park here.'

Morton glanced automatically though the window of his suite, towards the spot at the end of the car park where Clark had carefully parked his Jaguar thirty-six hours earlier. 'I found that he was proposing to carry on in the same way Sam Jackson had done. That was shocking, to me. That's why I asked him to meet me privately.'

'I think you should tell us what happened at this private meeting, don't you?'

He nodded, as casually as if he had been accepting a suggestion for a minor move on stage. 'Ernie wasn't as flamboyant as Sam had been, but he made it clear to me that he had all the information on the people in his cast that Sam had accumulated. He made it clear that he would blackmail people with their past sins just as unscrupulously, if he found it necessary to do so. That was his phrase. He said Sam had enjoyed being a bastard and that he wouldn't enjoy it, but he would behave like a bastard if necessary. He said I wasn't being realistic if I thought anything was going to change with Sam's death. That was when I decided that he would have to go. I'd never planned on that, but it became necessary.'

It was the sort of phrase they'd heard before from ruthless killers who had lost all moral sense. It came oddly from his amiable, grey-haired, seventy-three-year-old whom the media had installed as a national treasure. It was Bert Hook who took it upon himself to prompt the recital of the next part of the story. 'Mr Clark had a pistol.'

'Yes. He was absurdly proud of it. I think he enjoyed boasting about how he was bold enough to possess it. It's not usual in our game to be armed, you know. I think Ernie is the first man I've known in the world of drama who actually possessed a firearm and boasted that he'd be able to defend himself if necessary.'

'How long had he had it?'

Sir Bradley looked into Hook's rubicund, curiously innocent features and found them strangely reassuring. 'Certainly since we began filming the first episode of the Inspector Loxton series. Maybe longer than that. A Beretta, it was. As far as I know, he'd never fired the thing. He just seemed ridiculously pleased to have it. He called it his "little weakness" to me. I don't think many of the others even knew that he had such a weapon. Actors don't usually offer much of a physical threat – not to powerful men like producers. But he was quite vain about that pistol. When I asked if he still had it, he produced it from the glove box of the Jag. He showed me that it was loaded and where the safety catch was. Then he waved it about and said it was always available to him if people got above themselves and forgot who was really the boss.'

'So you took it from him.'

'I didn't have to. Ernie was so proud of it and the brilliant condition that it was in that he put it into my hands for me to examine it. Invited me to feel how naturally it sat there. He obviously didn't regard me as any sort of threat, you see.'

'No. He didn't know about your illness, I suppose.'

'He hadn't a clue about it, no. I remember thinking at that moment how convenient that was for me. It was almost as if someone had sent me there to do this. I pretended to examine the pistol admiringly, then slipped off the safety catch and shot him through the temple. It didn't seem to make a great deal of noise – nothing like as much as I'd expected.'

'And there was no one in the car park at the time.'

'It appears not, no. I was very lucky, wasn't I? But then, when you haven't long to live, that sort of luck doesn't matter much one way or the other.'

At a nod from Lambert, Hook stood up and delivered the formal words of arrest, on suspicion of the murders of Samuel Terence Jackson and Ernest Clark.

Sir Bradley Morton listened with careful interest and said, 'What happens now?'

'We take you into the station. You will be formally charged and asked to sign a statement in due course. After that, I am not quite certain what will happen.'

It was perfectly true. He had never arrested a man in circumstances even remotely similar to these. The law would take its inevitable course, presumably. But this proud, dignified, strangely certain man would not live long enough to endure a murder trial.

They took him down through the hotel reception area, where most of his fellow actors had assembled prior to departure. The old knight enjoyed his last small, dramatic scene. 'You're all off the hook now, in more ways than one. The police have their man and two mouths which could have been very harmful to you have been shut for ever. Dennis Potter gave me the idea, you know. We Forest of Dean boys know what's important, you see!'

And then he was gone, out between his captors and into the open air, leaving behind a suitably astonished range of faces at his final dramatic exit.